BROKEN IN LITTLE LEAF CREEK

A LITTLE LEAF CREEK COZY MYSTERY
BOOK TWENTY-THREE

CINDY BELL

Copyright © 2024 Cindy Bell

All rights reserved.

Cover Design by Lou Harper, Cover Affairs

All rights reserved. No part of this publication may be reproduced or transmitted in any form or by any means, electronic or mechanical, including photocopy, recording, or any information storage or retrieval system, without permission in writing from the publisher.

This is a work of fiction. The characters, incidents and locations portrayed in this book and the names herein are fictitious. Any similarity to or identification with the locations, names, characters or history of any person, product or entity is entirely coincidental and unintentional.

All trademarks and brands referred to in this book are for illustrative purposes only, are the property of their respective owners and not affiliated with this publication in any way. Any trademarks are being used without permission, and the publication of the trademark is not authorized by, associated with or sponsored by the trademark owner.

ISBN: 9798328442572

CHAPTER 1

"Tessa!" Cassie Alberta-Vail's voice carried through Tessa Watters' house.

"In the kitchen." Tessa turned around to see Cassie walk through the kitchen door. She didn't have the usual pep in her step. "What's wrong?"

"I'm just a bit tired and hungry." Cassie sat down on the closest kitchen chair and sniffed the air with a hopeful smile. "Is that blueberries I smell?"

"It was." Tessa winced and pointed at an empty saucepan. "I made a sauce to put on some pancakes this morning with the berries I had left. I'm sorry, I would have saved you some, but I wasn't expecting you for breakfast. You were on your honeymoon, and then you spent the last couple of mornings with your new hubby, so I've gotten out of the habit of having breakfast with you. It's great that you're here, though."

Cassie and her husband, Sebastian Vail, had gone to a small bed and breakfast in the mountains for a few nights for their honeymoon. It had been the perfect little getaway. But they had plans to go on a longer trip to celebrate when Sebastian could get more time away from his farm.

"I know, but since we've come back, Sebastian doesn't eat breakfast. He makes these weird green shakes in the morning. He claims they're so great and healthy, but I think most of it gets stuck in his teeth."

"You poor thing." Tessa laughed as she walked over to the fridge and opened the door. "I'm sure I have something in here you can eat. But I don't have much. I need to get to the store. And I have to go out soon, so I don't have a lot of time."

"It's all right. Don't worry about it. I also don't have much at home, aside from vegetables. I'll eat something at the diner. I don't have a shift today, but I can go get something." Cassie laughed at the thought of explaining to her boss at Mirabel's Diner, Mirabel Light, why she was eating there. She was sure she would find it amusing. "I know I'm being ridiculous."

"Are you?" Tessa looked her over from head to toe. "I can't have you wasting away on me. Sebastian should be taking better care of you."

"It's not his fault. He says I can eat whatever I want, but how do you tell someone who's drinking six different kinds of leafy greens you just want some bacon? Or waffles?" Cassie sighed again as she drifted lower in her chair. "Yes, waffles!"

"Cassie, you just tell him." Tessa handed her an apple and sat down in the chair beside her. "It's not waffles, but it's better than a vegetable drink."

"Thank you." Cassie had a bite.

"You two are married now. You can't be afraid to tell him the truth, or eat what you want. That'll drive you nuts."

"Maybe. I did try his drink. He was so happy to make it for me." Cassie lowered her voice and glanced toward the door. "It was terrible. It tasted like drinking mud from a garden."

"Oh, Cassie." Tessa laughed. "I hope you didn't tell him that. You don't have to be that honest."

"I didn't. But my face might have." Cassie scrunched up her nose. "I swear, he ate normal food before the wedding and when we were away."

"Maybe he's worried about getting out of shape now that he's married. He's probably just trying to impress you." Tessa winked at her as she stood up again. "Well, I have a great idea. I'm going to my friend Sheila's farm now to get some more blueberries. You can join me, then we'll stop and get you some real food after. The apple should tide you over till then. Then, tomorrow morning, you can come over for breakfast, and fill your belly with as many waffles and blueberries as you want."

"That sounds so good." Cassie jumped to her feet, and her eyes lit up with enthusiasm. "I can't wait."

"Then let's get going. I'm taking over one of my vanilla cakes. It's already in the jeep because I'm bringing the goats, so they can help trim back some overgrowth on Sheila's property."

"Ah, the best lawnmowers, huh?" Cassie followed after Tessa. For a moment her thoughts shifted back to the first few weeks she'd been Tessa's neighbor, and how she'd wondered if Tessa would actually leave her house that day. Now, they rarely got through a day without speaking to each other at some point.

"Exactly, here, you can help me wrangle them." Tessa dropped a few carrot pieces into Cassie's palm, then stepped out onto the front porch.

The goats barreled around the side of the house and ran straight toward them.

"All right, boys, all right, settle down. There're enough treats for both of you." Tessa hooked Gerry's leash on to his collar and guided him toward the jeep parked in the driveway.

Cassie attached Billy's leash and followed after Tessa. Once they had them both in the back of the jeep, Cassie gave Harry, Tessa's collie mix, a few treats. "We won't be long." She patted his head, then climbed into the passenger side.

"I think Harry will be happy for a break from the goats."

"Probably." Cassie buckled her seat belt. "So, you're exchanging goat labor for berries?"

"Not exactly." Tessa turned on the jeep and backed out of the driveway. "Sheila's been having some trouble lately. I'll pay for my berries, but she gets to borrow the goats for free." She turned onto a narrow side road. "I can't believe everything that's happening around town."

"What do you mean?" Cassie gazed out the window. The enchanting view of the farmland they passed by held most of her attention. It still surprised her that she'd gone from living in a luxurious penthouse to being back in a quaint little town that reminded her of her youth. Growing up in a small town had taught her many things, but since moving to Little Leaf Creek, she'd discovered that not all small towns were the same.

"You haven't heard?"

"No, what have I missed?" Cassie shifted her attention to Tessa, drawn in by the sudden rigidness of her friend's shoulders.

"There's been something very strange happening. Quite a few farmers have had their equipment stolen or damaged, including Sheila's small tractor. She had someone out to fix it, and the very next day it was stolen. Both the cost of the repairs and the cost of getting a replacement have set her back quite a bit. Her husband recently passed away, so she's having to do almost everything herself at the moment." Tessa turned down a long dirt driveway. "I'm not sure she's going to survive the season if this keeps up, and she's not the only one. Many farmers around here are hanging on by the skin of their teeth, so having any kind of extra cost can really put them at risk."

"I didn't know anything about that. I'm surprised Sebastian hasn't mentioned something." Cassie peered through the window at the small farmhouse Tessa parked in front of.

Tessa stepped out of the jeep and waved to a woman near a clothesline on the left-hand side of the house. "Hi, Sheila!"

Sheila added a few clothespins to the line to hold up a T-shirt, then turned to greet Tessa. "Oh, I'm so glad you're here." She laughed as the goats jumped out of the jeep. "And you, too, Tessa, of course."

"Don't worry. People are usually happier to see the goats than me." Tessa chuckled, then gestured to Cassie. "You know Cassie, don't you? She works at Mirabel's Diner."

"Oh, yes, and she stole the most eligible bachelor in town." Sheila raised her eyebrows as she smiled. "How could I not know you?"

"That seems to be what I'm famous for around here." Cassie laughed. "I'm pretty lucky to have him. That's for sure."

"I'm sure he feels the same way about you." Sheila winked at her, then shielded her eyes as she looked over her small farm. "The spots that need trimming the most are near my fence. I've been able to get pretty much everything else with the mower, but I just don't have the energy to tackle the fence line, and of course, Tom has been over here complaining. He doesn't even run the farm anymore and he's complaining all the time." She rolled her eyes. "Neighbors are the worst. I never complain when his boy is running that tractor at all hours of the morning, but let one weed creep through his fence and it's like the whole world is imploding."

"He's particular, eh?" Tessa nodded as she surveyed the fence. "I've known Tom for a long time. He's very proud of his farm. I'm sure it was hard for him to hand it down to his son, but it's a good thing he did."

"It is. Simon seems to be taking good care of things over there." Sheila glanced at Cassie.

"Don't you worry about Tom. My boys will have the whole area cleared out before he can even think about complaining again." Tessa guided the goats to the foliage, then took off their leashes.

"Wonderful." Sheila clasped her hands together as she smiled. "That will be such a relief, one less thing on my to-do list. And it looks like they've already started."

Cassie glanced around and noticed Gerry and Billy munching on the overgrown grass that lined the fence. "Looks like it." She laughed.

CHAPTER 2

"Why don't you both come up on the porch and have some iced tea with me. I just made it this morning. I'd love to hear about your days as a police officer, Tessa, if you're willing to share, and of course, I'm dying to hear about how you're enjoying married life, Cassie." Sheila led them up onto the side porch of the house.

"This is for you." Tessa handed her the cake.

"Oh, thank you. You know it's my favorite. I can't wait to have some later. But I had some pastries delivered with my bread this morning because I knew I would be having guests. I should have realized you would bring something. I'll be right back out with the tea and pastries. How does that sound?"

"Great. Thank you." Cassie passed her hand across her stomach as it rumbled. She'd been battling a few extra pounds lately, mainly because Tessa was such a great baker, and she couldn't resist one of her sweet treats. But at the moment she wanted nothing more than to eat exactly what she wanted instead of counting calories or chugging strange concoctions.

Sheila disappeared inside the house, and Cassie settled into one of the rocking chairs on the porch. She expected the chair beside her to be filled by Tessa, but she stood at the edge of the porch and gazed across the field of the neighboring farm.

"Do you see something interesting, Tessa?" Cassie stood up and walked over to join her.

"It's just odd that Simon's left his tractor in the middle of his farm like that. It's so far out from the house." Tessa settled her hands on her hips.

"Maybe he's in there taking a little break?" Cassie studied the vehicle. "Or he had to go and get something and he preferred to walk? He's probably coming right back."

"True. Still, it's not a good idea to leave anything unattended right now."

"I know Sebastian has been much more careful with his farm machinery since we've been back, but

I had no idea why. I wonder why he didn't tell me?"

"He probably just doesn't want you to worry, especially since nothing's happened on his farm." Tessa looked over at her. "Between the green juice and keeping this to himself, I'd guess he's a little nervous about his new role as a husband."

"What role? We've been together for quite a while. A piece of paper shouldn't make a difference."

"Maybe not to you, but even though he's still quite young, Sebastian was raised by his grandfather. I remember the man, though we didn't know each other well. My biggest impression of him was he was traditional. I always thought his influence was the reason why Sebastian didn't commit to someone for so long. Sebastian wasn't looking for just any person, he was looking for the one." Tessa shrugged as she smiled. "People don't often believe in that kind of thing anymore, and I'd say, I didn't believe it, either, until you showed up. When you went on a date with Ollie, I was a fan, of course—you're a wonderful person. But I also knew you didn't quite fit. You two would have butted heads at every turn. Ollie is a hard man to be with. Mirabel knows how to manage him. Sebastian may seem pretty easygoing and mild, but once he locked on to you I knew he wasn't letting go. So, if he's a little nervous, be patient with him. He's figuring out how to be the man every man before him has told him he should be."

Detective Oliver Graham was Tessa's late friend's son. Alice had passed away when Oliver was young, and Tessa had helped raise him and had been a mentor to him when he joined the police force, which had led to Tessa being shot in the leg while protecting him on a job. Cassie had become good friends with Oliver, who now dated Mirabel.

"But Sebastian doesn't have to be anything different from who he is." Cassie turned back toward the house. "I love him for exactly who he is."

"I know you do, and he'll figure that out, too, soon enough." Tessa patted her shoulder as the door to the house swung open.

Sheila stepped back outside with a large tray clasped in her hands.

"Let me help you with that." Cassie grinned as the tray wobbled. "I'm an expert."

"I bet you are." Sheila handed the tray over. "Thank you."

Cassie balanced it on one hand as she walked over to the large table in the center of the porch.

When she'd first taken on a job as a waitress, she'd been nervous she'd never get better at it. She'd worked as a waitress for a short time before she married her first husband, and when she'd moved to town she'd sort of fallen into the job at Mirabel's. But the more than twenty years that had passed left her body sore and her confidence stunted. Over time she'd gotten used to the work again.

Cassie set the tray down on the table, and after handing out the iced tea to Tessa and Sheila, she picked up a glass as well as a small plate with a cheese Danish on it. Her mouth watered at the sight of the pastry. She settled in the rocking chair and took a bite.

"Don't forget your berries, Tessa. I made sure you would have plenty. I can't wait to see what you do with them this time." Sheila settled into her own chair. "I'm so glad you're sharing your baking skills with us. You two are so lucky to be neighbors. I wish I had neighbors like you, instead of neighbors who want to cause me trouble."

"I'm not sure if you would be saying that if you were my neighbor. Cassie has had more than a few run-ins with my goats. They aren't always the most polite creatures." Tessa's mind flooded with some of their antics.

"This is so delicious." Cassie licked her lips, then smiled at Tessa. "Your goats are definitely adventurous, but I do love having them around."

"I'm glad you do. I'm not sure the rest of the neighbors on our street would agree." Tessa laughed. "But at least they can be useful in some ways."

"Speaking of your goats." Cassie surveyed the fence line as she took another bite of the pastry. "Where are they?"

"Where are they?" Tessa sat forward in her chair. "What do you mean? They should be hard at work." She scanned the area, then sighed. "Oh dear, where did they run off to?" She laughed as she shook her head. "I'm sorry, Sheila, I guess they had enough of the grass and decided to get a taste of something else."

"Oh no, my laundry!" Sheila's eyes widened. "Do you think they're chewing it up?"

"I'd love to say no." Tessa groaned as Cassie took off at a run toward the clothesline behind the house.

"Tessa, what if they get to my delicates?" Sheila gasped, then burst into laughter. "That would be pretty funny, wouldn't it?"

"I suppose it would, but let's just hope they

haven't eaten everything and the whole clothesline with it." Tessa flinched as she imagined the destruction taking place. "I'm so sorry. They don't usually walk away from a good pile of grass. Something must have caught their attention."

"It's okay." Cassie's voice carried around the corner of the house. "The clothes are safe, and I think I see the goats."

"Great." Tessa made her way toward Cassie's voice. As a breeze rushed across the field beside Sheila's house, Tessa caught the faint scent of strawberries. If the goats had caught a whiff of that delicious smell, she doubted they would be easy to wrangle. She quickened her pace to catch up with Cassie.

"They're not getting into too much trouble, are they, Cassie?" Tessa shielded her eyes from the morning sunlight and spotted Cassie midway through the field of the neighboring property. "Are they with you, Cassie? Do you have them?"

Cassie stood frozen in the middle of the field. She didn't call out to Tessa. Her shoulders remained tight and high. The only movement was the breeze fluttering through strands of her hair as she stared at the tractor parked in front of her.

"Cassie!" A mixture of confusion and frustration

combined with the pain in Tessa's leg as she rushed toward Cassie.

Finally, Cassie turned to look over her shoulder with wide eyes. Her lips moved without a sound slipping past.

Tessa's heart raced. Something was wrong. Tessa quickened her pace to reach Cassie's side.

Cassie finally found her voice. "Call Ollie, Tessa. You need to call Ollie."

"Cassie, what is it?" Tessa took a step closer to her and spotted the goats huddled on the other side of the tractor.

The lifeless body of a man was sprawled out on the ground beside the bleating goats. Blood stained the grass surrounding his head.

CHAPTER 3

Tessa dug her phone out of her pocket. She dialed Oliver's number and raised the phone to her ear as she scanned the area for any clues.

"Ollie, you need to get out to Tom's farm, and fast. Someone's dead."

A barrage of questions followed Tessa's statement, but she barely heard any of them as she ended the call. Her mind filled with an assessment of every tiny detail about the man who lay before her. Clearly the head injury had taken his life. But could it have been an accident, or was it murder? Her first assumption was murder, but with a critical eye she surveyed his surroundings for any indication of a tragic accident.

"Cassie, did you see anyone?" Tessa looked up into Cassie's eyes and found her still dazed by the shock of discovering the body. "Cassie." She snapped her fingers just to the side of her head. "Did you see anyone?"

Cassie blinked hard. She licked her lips as she heaved a heavy sigh. "No. No, I didn't see anyone. I just saw the goats and came over here to get them, but when I looked past the tractor, I saw him." Her voice cracked. "Who would do that to him?"

"So, you don't think it was an accident, either?" Tessa stood a few feet from the tractor, so she didn't contaminate the scene, as she paced slowly from side to side. "Oh, look at that. I can see traces of blood on the front here." She pointed toward the curve. "But I can't picture how he could have slipped and hit his head that hard."

"No." Cassie's voice took on a hard edge as she tried to catch her breath. "No, I think someone must have killed him. I think it's pretty clear from his injuries that someone did this on purpose."

"Okay, all right now. Just breathe, nice and slow."

"Who did this?" Cassie's gaze suddenly swung around the expansive farmland. "Are they still nearby?"

Sirens wailed from the road.

"If they are, they won't be for long. They'll hear those sirens and run," Tessa mumbled under her breath as she pulled her phone out of her pocket. "I should have told Ollie to come in quiet."

Cassie shooed the goats away from the area. "No wonder they ran off. They must have been curious about this."

"We need to keep them away from the crime scene. They've already contaminated it, but hopefully not too much."

"Tessa!" Oliver broke into a jog toward them.

As Tessa turned to look at him, she noticed Sheila stood at her fence staring across the field as other officers began arriving.

"What happened?" Oliver stopped beside them, then his gaze settled on the body. "That's Richard. Richard Lawson."

"Oh, of course. I thought I recognized him," Tessa said.

Oliver's eyes narrowed as he crouched down beside the body and checked for a pulse. "I've been looking into him. I spoke with him early this morning." His focus shifted to the tractor. "It looks like he struck his head there. But it doesn't look like this was an accident. It looks like someone slammed his head into the front." He straightened up and shouted a few commands to the officers who approached him. "Who found him?" He looked between Tessa and Cassie. His gray eyes sharp and demanding.

"They did." Cassie pointed to the goats who snacked on the grass nearby.

"Funny, Cassie. Who really found him?" Oliver's tight expression softened as he drank in the sight of her pale skin and tight lips. "Are you okay? You found him, didn't you?"

"They found him. I wasn't joking. I followed them over here and that's when I saw him. They must have walked through the gate just like I did." Cassie pointed to an open gate in the fence that separated the properties. "I didn't see anyone else. I don't know anything more than that."

Officers started cordoning off the scene.

"What about Sheila?" Oliver gestured to the woman who stood with one of the officers at the fence line. "Did she see anything?"

"I don't know. She didn't mention anything." Tessa stared across the field at her. "We came here to get berries from her, and to let the goats trim some of the foliage. We saw the tractor sitting off on its own so far out in the field and thought it was strange, but we didn't know Richard was out here. We couldn't see him because of the tractor."

"All right, I'll speak to Sheila." Oliver looked back at Cassie.

The goats bolted over to Tessa and sniffed at her hands and pockets in search of treats. When they found none, Billy tried to sniff Oliver's hand and Gerry stamped one hoof against the ground, then scraped it back over the grass a few times. Oliver peered down at the ground by Gerry. He bent down, then looked up at Tessa. As he met her eyes, he smiled slightly. "It looks like Gerry just gave me our first possible clue."

"What do you mean? What do you have there?" Tessa peered at what Oliver was putting into an evidence bag.

"It looks like some sort of material, some cloth." Oliver surveyed Richard's body from a distance. "It doesn't look like it came from Richard's clothing, but I'll have to have a closer look."

"You said you spoke with him this morning and were investigating him? What for?" Cassie asked.

"We'll get to that. Let me get some answers first. How long were you two at Sheila's farm before you found him?" Oliver jotted a note down.

"Not long." Tessa looked in the direction of the body. "It doesn't look like there was a fight."

"You're right. But the medical examiner will be able to tell us more." Oliver wrote another note, then looked up at Tessa. "Are you sure you didn't hear anything? No argument? No shouting?"

"I'm sure." Tessa looked him straight in the eyes. "I think he must have been dead before we arrived, otherwise I'm sure we would have heard something."

"It looks like he died within the last hour or two. But the medical examiner will have to confirm that, of course," Oliver said.

"I only found him because the goats wandered over here." Cassie tilted her head to the side as she studied the goats. "Which is actually pretty strange."

"You're right, it is." Tessa followed the path they took. "They won't usually leave a good meal, unless it's for a treat. But I did smell strawberries. Maybe they came over here looking for them."

"Over there." Oliver pointed to a container of strawberries that had been spilled over beside a toolbox on the ground nearby.

"Maybe Richard was snacking on them?" Tessa suggested.

"Why was Richard here if this farm belongs to

Simon? Why would he be eating berries?" Cassie asked.

"Richard is a farm equipment supplier. He also does repairs. I know Simon had asked him to come out here this morning to work on the tractor." Oliver pointed to a toolbox. "It looks like he was fixing whatever was wrong."

"So, maybe he took a little break?" Cassie suggested.

"Maybe." Tessa eyed the strawberries. "Maybe he was paid in berries. How did you know he was out here?"

"Richard mentioned to me that he had to come here, so he cut our conversation short. I was investigating an accusation against him for arson. His late father's good friend, Candy, claims Richard set fire to her car because his father, Wyatt, left it to her instead of him. It was a classic and Richard was furious about it."

"And do you think Richard did it?" Tessa asked.

"No." Oliver shook his head. "It was ruled an accidental fire, but I had to look into it and take Candy's accusation seriously."

"Do you think she might have done this?" Tessa asked. "Maybe to get revenge?"

"She wasn't in the area as far as I know. She

works and lives a few hours away. Yesterday, when I spoke to the officer Candy reported the complaint to, he said she was at their station. But she could have made it here in time to commit the murder, I guess. I'll obviously look into it." Oliver glanced in the direction of the body.

"We'll leave you to it." Tessa patted his arm as she stepped past him. "I need to get the goats out of here before they destroy anything."

"Let me know if you come across anything else on them that might be evidence," Oliver said as she began wrangling the goats.

"I'll give them a thorough inspection." Tessa attached Gerry's leash and Cassie did the same with Billy's, then they guided them back toward the fence line.

The officer who'd been speaking with Sheila walked past them and out to the crime scene.

Tessa nodded to Sheila when she reached her.

"The officer told me what you found. Do you know who it is?" Sheila's voice trembled. "Not Simon, I hope."

"No, not Simon." Cassie cleared her throat. "Ollie identified him as Richard Lawson. Did you know him?"

"Yes, he's fixed some of the machinery before.

But I didn't know him well." Sheila lowered her voice and stepped closer to Tessa. "I don't want to point any fingers, but I know someone who had a big problem with Richard." She narrowed her eyes. "His name is Lewis Cole. I'm not saying he's a murderer, but I've heard him complaining about Richard loudly. He was so angry with him."

"Thanks, that's a good place for us to start. Is there anyone else you think might have had a hand in this?" Tessa asked.

"No, I can't think of anyone." Sheila shook her head.

"If you do think of anything, make sure you let me know." Tessa cast a glance toward Oliver as he and his team continued to evaluate the scene. "Ollie will have some questions for you. You really should tell him about Lewis, and if you think of anyone else you might suspect. Anyone you might have seen hanging around Simon's farm, anything like that."

"Sure, of course I will. I hope the killer is found soon. I can't believe this happened right next door." Sheila scanned the neighboring property.

CHAPTER 4

Cassie threw Harry a ball in Tessa's front yard as shouting and bleating drifted from behind the house.

Tessa dusted off her hands as she walked around the side of the house, shaking her head.

"They gave you quite a fight, huh?" Cassie looked over at her. When they'd arrived at Tessa's house there was a small section of fence that Sebastian had begun replacing because the goats were starting to get through it. They were skilled escape artists.

"They don't like being locked in their pen at all. They're definitely used to being free-roaming goats. I'll just pop Harry in there with them. That should keep them all entertained." Tessa ushered Harry toward the back, then walked over to Cassie. "I couldn't find any other possible evidence on the goats." Tessa continued toward her jeep. "Sheila gave us a good tip and I'd like to follow up on it."

"Shouldn't we wait and let Ollie talk to Lewis first?" Cassie hesitated as Tessa climbed into the driver's seat.

"We should, yes. But we're not going to." Tessa paused as she slid the key into the ignition. Her eyes met Cassie's. "At least, I'm not going to. Whatever crime spree has erupted in our little town, I want it brought to an end. Ollie has his way of doing things, and I have mine."

"You're right. We need to do something." Cassie settled in the passenger seat. "Do you know Lewis well?"

"I do. He's lodged complaints against just about everyone in this town at some time or another, and has often had a problem with my goats. But I must say he has a soft spot for his horses." Tessa backed out of the driveway. "I'd like to say I don't think he's a murderer, but he strikes me as the type who could easily snap under the right kind of pressure."

"Okay, so we need to find out what he knows."

"He doesn't live far." Tessa turned down the main road, then took a right onto a side street. "The goats once ate his flower bed. I can't really blame him for being angry. But he wasn't just angry, he was irate, as he has been for every little thing that has ever been done to him. He has some kind of anger problem. Which makes me wonder if he could have lost his temper with Richard." She turned into a driveway and parked the jeep. "Let's find out."

Tessa led the way up the short walkway to the front door of the one-story house. Dark green paint had faded over the years into a paler shade. The short overhang above the front door sagged a little under the weight of many rainy seasons.

Tessa knocked on the door, then stepped back as she glanced at Cassie and whispered, "We're not going to push too hard. Got it?"

"Got it." Cassie nodded as she positioned herself close to Tessa.

The door opened, revealing a tall, thick man who looked to be in his fifties. His gaze skipped over Cassie, then settled on Tessa as he squinted at her. "Come to pay me back for that garden your goats destroyed?"

"That was several years ago, and I already paid you more than enough to cover it." Tessa's tone remained stern as she continued. "I'm here to speak to you about something much more serious."

"Oh?" Lewis put his hands in his pockets. "What's that?"

"Richard Lawson was found dead today, out on Tom's farm. Have you heard?" Tessa asked.

"No, I didn't hear anything about that. Isn't that Simon's farm now?" Lewis cleared his throat. "Richard was getting up there in age, I guess, but he wasn't that old. A heart attack?"

"No." Tessa's voice tightened. "He was murdered."

"Oh." Lewis' eyes widened as he nodded. "I guess that makes more sense."

"It makes more sense to you that a man would be murdered? Why is that?" Cassie asked.

"He was an easy man to want dead." Lewis shrugged. "I'm sure he had plenty of enemies."

"Like who?" Tessa shifted closer to him.

"I can't give you any particular names. But if you want to know why someone would want to kill him, I can tell you that." Lewis shot a sharp look over his shoulder, then looked back at them. "But whatever I say must stay between us, I don't want the cops knowing my name, and I don't want anybody in town knowing I said something."

Cassie was intrigued to hear what he might have

to share. She nodded to him as she leaned closer to hear every word.

"Tell me everything you know." Tessa looked him straight in the eye.

"I'm not one to go around badmouthing people. I give everybody a fair shake, but once they cross me, I never forget it." Lewis' tone hardened. "Richard sold me my own stolen horse trailer as if it was something he just came across. I told him it was mine, but he insisted it wasn't."

"Did you go to the police? He shouldn't have been able to get away with that," Cassie said.

"Yes, of course I did. But it had a different VIN on it, so they said I couldn't do anything about it." Lewis sneered.

"If it had a different number, then it was probably a different trailer. If it was the same make and model, then it probably just looked similar. Did you consider that you might be the one making a mistake?" Tessa asked.

"Not for a second. I know my trailer. I know every dent and ding on it, every bit of scraped paint. It was mine. He stole it and sold it back to me." Lewis leaned against the doorway and stared hard at Tessa. "I even had the guy on one of my cameras. I told the police that, but they still wouldn't help me. Said the image was too blurry and that they couldn't prove anything because it didn't show him actually stealing it."

"I still think it's possible that you were mistaken. Maybe you just wanted to be right, so you saw every nick and blemish as identical to your old one. Our minds can play tricks on us sometimes." Cassie tapped on the side of her head.

"If you don't want to hear what I have to say, then don't listen. If you don't want to believe me, don't believe me. But I know everything about my farm equipment. I know that's what he sold me. But when I told him that, he insisted he didn't know anything about it being stolen and he even accused me of trying to swindle him. He refused to give me my money back. He offered to switch them, but why would I pay for any trailer when he stole mine in the first place? I shouldn't have to pay anything to get mine back." Lewis' veins throbbed in his forehead as his cheeks reddened.

Cassie realized that he was furious, and that kind of anger could translate into committing murder. Was he the one who'd killed Richard? She thought it was a definite possibility.

"All right, all right, calm down. I believe you,

but he never admitted to stealing it?" Tessa raised her eyebrows.

"No, of course he didn't admit to stealing it. He just acted like I'd lost my mind, and the police wouldn't do anything about it. He just continued to refuse to give me my money back."

"That must have made you so angry." Cassie studied him closely as he shifted from one foot to the other and smacked his fist against his open palm.

"Of course it did. But I didn't have a choice. I just had to deal with it. There was nothing else I could do." Lewis let his hands fall back to his sides.

"Did he ever tell you where he'd gotten your stolen trailer?" Tessa asked.

"When he said he hadn't stolen it, I demanded to know where he got it from. He claimed someone had sold it to him and he fixed it up a bit, but he wouldn't tell me who. He said he didn't want me showing up there ranting about it and losing it. I don't doubt for a second he did all of it himself. There have been rumors going around that he's been sabotaging things on the farms all around this area, so that he can get money from repairing or replacing them, and everyone just keeps hiring him. Well, I guess they can't anymore." Lewis laughed and shook his head. "I know it's not funny. I'm sorry, I don't know why I laughed."

As Cassie watched a cloud of frustration build within Lewis' eyes, she believed her first instinct was right. He could definitely be angry enough to be the murderer.

"The two of you better not be concocting some story that paints me in a bad light." Lewis' tone took on a gruff edge.

"No one is concocting anything. But I'm sure the police are going to be by soon enough to ask you some questions. Your best bet is to cooperate with them." Tessa's gaze lingered on his tense expression. "And try not to laugh."

"I'm sure I can count on you to dispel any rumors I might be involved in this?" Lewis passed a glare between the two of them. "I'm sure that's what led you here in the first place."

"Did you have the names of anyone we should suspect?" Cassie's gaze locked to his. "You said he probably had a lot of enemies, but the only one you told us about is you."

"I knew it. I knew that's why you came here. You think I killed him," Lewis huffed.

"We came here because we want to help find out

the truth about what exactly happened to Richard," Tessa said.

"The truth is I had nothing to do with the murder, and I have nothing more to say. So, get out of here." Lewis tilted his head toward the street.

"Okay. We'll be on our way, but we'll be back if we have any more questions." Tessa gestured for Cassie to walk ahead of her.

Despite Tessa's fairly small size, she had a confidence and authority that always made Cassie feel safe even around the most intimidating people. "Well, what do you think?" Cassie slid into the passenger seat of the jeep.

"I think he was very angry, and that kind of anger can turn to murder." Tessa turned on the jeep and eased out of Lewis' driveway. "I also think we need to be careful. The closer we get to the killer, the more panicked that person is going to be."

"Okay. Noted."

"I'm going to reach out to Mark and see if he can help me out with any insight into whether Lewis' claims of his horse trailer being stolen and Richard selling it back to him could be true. Mark usually has his finger on the pulse of any criminal activity around here." Tessa held up her hand before Cassie could open her mouth. "And no comments about it. It's a professional call, not a romantic one."

"All right, I won't say a word." Cassie smiled at the mention of Mark Collingswood, a local lawyer and Tessa's old friend.

Cassie began to run through what they knew about the murder so far, as Tessa drove back toward their houses.

"So, we suspect Richard might have been killed because he was engaging in unsavory, possibly illegal business practices." Cassie glanced over at Tessa. "If it wasn't Lewis, as he claims, do you think someone else would have been angry enough over a business transaction to do this to Richard?"

"I think money is tight for everyone at the moment, and we're not just talking about making ends meet. Many farm owners are on the verge of losing their livelihood and their homes. There's a lot at stake. If Richard swindled the wrong person, and they stood to lose everything because of it, then yes, I do think there's a good chance they murdered him. I think talking to Mark is a good first step, but from there, we really need to find out more about Richard's personal life and who he might have encountered in the past day or two. Those people are going to be our best suspect pool to start with."

Tessa turned into her driveway and put the jeep in park.

"I need to do a few things at home and get a new notebook. It's almost finished, and then I'll come over. I'll be quick. Sebastian is working." Cassie always wrote lists and notes, especially when she was investigating something, which seemed to be quite often due to her naturally curious nature and the fact that there always seemed to be some sort of mystery in Little Leaf Creek.

"Okay, I'll call Mark while you're doing that."

CHAPTER 5

After sending Sebastian a text to let him know what was happening, hanging the washing outside, getting changed because it was hotter than she thought it would be, and grabbing a new notebook, Cassie hurried across the driveway and through Tessa's gate, eager to get to the bottom of Richard's murder. She spotted the goats moving in slow circles around the pen. She guessed they were trying to find a way to escape, and it would be only a matter of time before they succeeded. She walked over and threw them a few carrot pieces, then she started up Tessa's porch stairs. She pushed the front door open, and Harry came running over as she stepped inside. "Hi, buddy." She rubbed behind his ears and called out, "Tessa."

"Come in, come in!" Tessa's voice drifted from the kitchen as she turned to look at her. "You still haven't really eaten, have you?" She clucked her tongue as she set down a plate with a grilled cheese sandwich onto the kitchen table. "It's all I could put together with what I have, but I know it's one of your favorites. Sit, eat, and I'll tell you what Mark told me."

"Thank you so much." Cassie dropped into a chair. She'd already started eating when Tessa began speaking.

"Mark's doing some more digging, but he was able to tell me Richard has been the subject of a few complaints, and they're not just from Lewis." Tessa sat down at the table as Cassie finished the food in her mouth.

"So, Lewis was telling us the truth."

"Maybe, or maybe just part of the truth. Just because Richard had complaints against him, that doesn't mean they were proven. Also, it doesn't absolve Lewis of the murder. In fact, it still includes him as a good suspect, I think. The problem is we have no proof of that."

Cassie wiped her mouth with a napkin, then put it on the table, and picked up her pen. "We need to focus on what we know, not what we think." She pulled her notebook out of her purse.

"To me it looked like someone had to have a lot of anger to kill Richard that way. Something had to be brewing. But it's just a hunch, and you know I like to operate on proof and facts."

"Maybe it's just a hunch, but it comes from years of experience, Tessa, from your wisdom. I give that a lot of credit."

"It isn't like the murderer just happened upon him on the side of the road. He was in the middle of a field. They had to go quite a distance to get to him. Maybe they were looking for him." Tessa looked at her phone as it beeped with a text. "It's from Mark. He was able to get Richard's phone records. He says there are no calls indicating someone was trying to find him. That's surprising." She looked up at Cassie. "So, if whoever did this didn't bother to call him first, they didn't want to talk, necessarily. They had no interest in working things out."

"And perhaps they even planned this." Cassie considered the possibility. "The killer might have thought it would look suspicious if their phone number was on Richard's phone around the time he died. Not just that, but if they did plan this, then they picked a time when they knew he would be out in the middle of the field, and maybe they knew no one else would be around."

"That's very true. So the question is, who knew he was going to be on that farm? If we can figure that out, that might narrow our suspect list down a bit. And, if the murder was planned, then this was personal, Richard knew his killer. But we still have to prove that."

"You're right. I don't think a stranger did this. I'll make a note of that. We may not have proof, but we have enough suspicion to lean on it as a good theory." Cassie jotted a note down in her notebook. "Was Richard married?"

"No, he lived alone. He recently took over his father's business after he'd worked there for years. He had no family or love interest as far as I know. There were rumors he had an affair with a married woman a couple of years ago and it didn't work out and he was heartbroken, so he hasn't dated since. But I don't know who the woman was or if it's true. After his father died, he worked alone without a business partner or employees."

"I wonder who would know his schedule." Cassie had a bite of the sandwich.

"Maybe no one. Maybe no one else knew what

he was up to at any given time. But we know Simon called him out to the farm this morning."

"So, you think he might be the murderer?" Cassie scrunched up her nose. "He had to know he would be the top suspect, though."

"He's definitely a suspect due to the murder happening on his property and knowing Richard would be there. But the people he might have told that he had asked Richard to come out to the farm this morning, will also enter our suspect pool. Unless we ask Simon, though, we won't know who they might be. And, of course, anyone could have seen Richard go out there or saw his truck out front and known he was there."

"Simon might have told quite a few people. And Richard could have told people he was going out there," Cassie suggested.

"Let's hope they didn't tell too many people or our suspect list is going to be very long."

Cassie finished off her sandwich. "This is so good. Thank you so much. I think we should get over to Simon's farm and talk to him."

"Let's hit the road." Tessa picked up her plate and grabbed a bottle of water out of the fridge. "Something to wash it down with."

"Thank you."

"All right, let's get going. The sooner we get some direction on this investigation, the better. With all the rumors that will be flying around town, it might become harder to sort out the truth from fiction." Tessa led the way out to the jeep.

Bleats from the backyard followed after them to the driveway.

"The poor goats. They don't like being cooped up in that pen. Sebastian said he'll be over later to fix the fence."

"That's if they don't figure their way out of the pen first." Cassie settled into the passenger seat. "I give them an hour."

"You're probably right, but I did some extra reinforcing this time." Tessa started the jeep and backed out of the driveway. She rolled down the road in the same direction they'd traveled that morning.

CHAPTER 6

Tessa parked in front of the small farmhouse and looked around the large, mostly empty yard. "It looks like the police have cleared out. I suppose there wasn't much evidence to collect." She stepped out of the jeep and looked toward the house. "I can see people moving around inside, though, so someone is home."

"There are two cars parked around the back of the house." Cassie walked over to Tessa. "Do you think Simon is going to want to talk to us after everything he's been through today?"

"Maybe not Simon. I don't really know him. But Tom and Pearl will speak to me. That's if they're here. They moved into a small house near town when Simon took over the farm, and Simon's fiancée is moving to Little Leaf Creek and into the farmhouse when they get married later in the year."

"All right, you lead the way, then. I'll hang back." Cassie waited as Tessa approached the farmhouse.

Moments later, Tessa knocked on the thick wooden door.

A woman in her seventies opened the door. Her red-rimmed blue eyes settled on Tessa.

"Surprise, surprise." Pearl sighed as she swung it open a little farther. "You might as well come in and accuse my poor boy of this horrible crime, too."

"Not at all, Pearl, not at all." Tessa sensed the tension brewing just beyond the door.

"Who is it, Mom?" A stern voice carried from inside the house. "Don't talk to anyone. Just say, 'No comment.'" Simon pulled the door the rest of the way open and glared at Cassie and Tessa.

"Easy, Simon. They're not reporters." Pearl pressed her hand against the chest of a man about Cassie's age who threatened to step right out onto the porch with them. "You know Tessa."

Simon squinted at her from behind silver, thin-framed glasses. "Yes, of course."

Pearl looked past Tessa, at Cassie, and nodded. "And Cassie."

"Cassie?" Simon looked her over. "You work at the diner, right?"

"Right." Cassie recognized both him and Pearl. Simon was a regular and she'd seen Pearl in there a couple of times. "We just wanted to check in on all of you, to make sure you're doing okay. I'm sure it was a shock after what happened to Richard."

"Quite a shock." A deeper, graveled voice spoke up from behind the mother and son. Because of his short stature they nearly blocked him from view.

"I came from the store to drop off some things for Simon and found the police all over the place." Pearl grabbed her neck as her voice shook. "It's just horrible."

"I'm sure. It must be terrible. All we want is to help get this figured out as fast as possible, so we can all find a way to move on." Tessa stepped farther into the house. She peered past Pearl and Simon. "Tom, was it your old tractor Richard was working on?"

"No, it wasn't." Simon spoke up. "I got rid of that when I took over. I bought one from Richard to replace it. He assured me it was in good shape. But today was the third time I had to call him out here to work on it."

"You never should have gotten rid of mine.

Wasn't nothing wrong with it," Tom mumbled as he looked at his son and shook his head.

"I know, Dad. I know!" Simon rolled his eyes. "You've made it very clear this is all my fault."

"If you just listened to me, boy, none of this would have happened!" Tom's voice raised as he glared at his son who stood at least a head taller, though had a slimmer frame than his father.

"Stop it, Tom, just stop it." Pearl grabbed her husband by the arm. "You're upsetting him! Come along, I'll get you some lemonade so you can cool off." She escorted him toward the kitchen.

Simon stared hard at the floor. "I can't believe this happened."

"Was Richard upset when he came here?" Tessa asked.

"I didn't even see him. I knew I needed to tend to the stock in the other field." Simon pointed in the direction of the field. "So, I left the keys in the tractor. It's not like anyone could steal it—it was broken. I couldn't get it to move. I told Richard all about it yesterday when I arranged for him to come out. I was out in the other field with my father when the police came to tell me what had happened."

"Did you notice anyone around? Hear anything?" Tessa asked.

"No, nothing." Simon shook his head.

"You must have been so frustrated to have to call Richard out here again, especially with your father breathing down your neck like that." Tessa tried to look into his eyes. "It's okay. You know this isn't your fault, don't you?"

"I guess. I mean, I did call him out here, didn't I? And yes, I was mad I had to call him out again to work on the tractor he claimed to have fixed two days before. You know, I used to take my car to this one mechanic. Everyone said he was so reliable, such a great guy, did such a great job on their cars. But every single time I took my car in for a repair, it ended up with a new problem within a week. I thought, well, it's just an old car, these things happen and so I kept going back to this mechanic and it kept happening. That's when my mother said to me, why don't you take it somewhere else? I said, what are you talking about? This guy's great. Everybody loves him. He does a great job. He gets the car in and out every time. Why would I need to go to anyone else? She said he always fixes the problem you bring it in for but who's to say he's not making the problem you have to bring it back for? People have to live, and some of them will make money any way they can. I thought she was being paranoid, to be honest with you. I really thought she was just being paranoid. There was no way this great guy would be doing something like that to me."

Tessa and Cassie stood in silence as he continued talking, hoping he'd reveal a clue.

"But I took it to another mechanic to appease her, because she wouldn't let up about it. He said the belts had been worn down intentionally. He told me my mechanic had been doing exactly what my mother had warned me he was doing. Of course, I never went back to that mechanic, and when things started happening like this with Richard and the tractor I bought from him, it felt very familiar. Again, my mother warned me he was probably scamming me, but I wanted to give him one more chance because I'd known Richard for a long time. I would even have called him a friend. His dad was very well respected in the community. Everyone around here has known Richard for a long time. I knew it wouldn't be easy to get other people to believe what he was doing, so I wanted to get some proof. I had another mechanic come look at the tractor yesterday to find out what the problem was. I wanted to see if Richard would come up with the same answer and actually get him to fix it properly. I gave him the chance and now I really regret it. I can't help thinking if I hadn't called him to come out here this morning, if I hadn't been so angry and insisted he come so early, maybe he would still be alive. I know it's not my fault. I didn't hurt the man. But someone did, and they did it on my property. He was here because I called him." He looked into Tessa's eyes as tears began to fill his own.

Tessa remained silent for a long moment. She wanted to reassure him, but after hearing his longwinded speech about what he suspected Richard of doing, she couldn't help but wonder if the tears were all an act, and he might be responsible for killing him.

CHAPTER 7

"You're doing the right thing by talking to us, Simon." Cassie took a step closer to him. "Who else might have known Richard would be here this morning?"

"No one that I know of. Unless he told someone. I didn't tell anyone. I didn't even tell my parents. I guess I was embarrassed that me buying a tractor had led to all these problems and that Richard was out here again trying to fix it. I really don't have anything more to say about it." Simon took a step back as his breathing quickened. "I already said too much. I've been telling my parents to be careful what they say, but I'm not taking my own advice."

"Wait. Wait just a second." Tessa held up her

hand. "You said you had another mechanic out here yesterday, right?"

Simon nodded.

"Did you tell him what your plan was?" Tessa asked.

"Yes, I did. And I might have said something to him about wanting to see what Richard had to say about it in the morning. But he had no reason to want to hurt Richard." Simon shrugged. "I don't think they even really knew each other."

"His name?" Tessa asked.

"Dean Moss. That's all I have to say about it." Simon ushered them back toward the door.

"Thanks for your help." As Cassie turned around, she noticed a piece of paper on the floor near a small table by the front door. As she reached down and picked it up, she read that it was a receipt from a bakery in Rombsby with today's date on it. Rombsby was a larger neighboring town. She handed it to Simon.

"Thank you." Simon placed it on the table.

"If you think of anything else that might help, of course contact the police, but if there's anything you want to tell us, we're willing to listen." Tessa stepped through the door.

"I won't be saying another word. I'm innocent, and I'm going to stay out of this as much as possible." Simon closed the door behind them.

"Well, that didn't go too well." Tessa climbed into the jeep.

"No, but it was interesting." Cassie sat down in the passenger seat. "It seems like even though Simon appeared to be upset by Richard's murder, he had every reason to be angry at him."

"I agree. I think he should be at the top of the suspect list." Tessa started the engine.

"We should see if we can find Dean."

"I think I know what shop he works out of. It's in Rombsby." Tessa turned onto another road and waved to a woman walking her small dog.

"That's Elena, right?" Cassie turned to look as the jeep rolled past. "She's fairly new here, isn't she?"

"Yes, she moved in about a month ago. And look at me making an effort to be friendly. Harry loves playing with Trixie, Elena's Pomeranian, at the dog park." Tessa merged onto the highway to Rombsby.

"You know how Sheila got a delivery from a bakery? Well, that piece of paper I picked up off Simon's floor was a receipt from today from the bakery in Rombsby. Maybe the person who dropped off the stuff saw something."

"That's possible. We'll have to look into that." Tessa pulled into the parking lot of a mechanic's shop. She parked near the only door and stepped out of the jeep. "As far as I know, Dean is employed here. Whether he's working today or not, we'll have to find out." She walked up to the door and peeked through the small, dirty window. "I don't see anyone inside."

The screech of an engine drew their attention to the open garage doors beside them.

"Someone's working. That's for sure." Tessa stepped through one of the open doors. "Hello? Is Dean here?"

"What are you looking for me for?" A young man in his twenties stepped out of the garage. He pulled a greasy bandana from his head as he looked between them.

"Dean, we're here about Richard Lawson." Tessa kept her tone casual. "We're looking into his death."

"What do you mean his death?" Dean wrung the bandana between his hands.

Cassie noticed tears and holes in Dean's T-shirt.

She glanced away when he followed her gaze down to his shirt.

"I know it doesn't look the best." Dean tugged at his T-shirt. "It's practically new, if you can believe it. The work I do is hard, and it's easy for things to get ripped up. And the cars don't care what I wear." He gave a short laugh.

"Of course." Cassie blushed.

"Do you know that Richard Lawson was found dead this morning on Simon's farm?" Tessa asked.

"He was?" Dean's eyes widened. "I had no idea."

"From what we understand you were out at that farm yesterday with Simon?" Tessa kept her voice even.

"Yeah, I was there." Dean shrugged. "Simon called me out there. He said he wanted a second opinion first, before Richard had a chance to get his hands on the tractor again."

"Did he tell you why that was?" Cassie watched as he stretched the bandana tight in his hands.

"I don't care about the details. I just do the job I get paid for."

"He suspected Richard might have been damaging the equipment, forcing Simon to pay him to come back out and repair it. Isn't that right?" Tessa asked.

"Well, I think you would have to ask Simon about that, wouldn't you?" Dean narrowed his eyes. "All I know is he asked me to come out and look at the tractor. I saw it had low oil but no evidence of a leak. I told Simon the leak had to be somewhere under the engine, and the whole thing would have to be pulled out and checked to see what needed to be fixed or replaced. He said Richard had just replaced part of the engine for the same problem. I told him I would check it for him and get it done that day. But he said he would take the issue up with Richard. Honestly, it was a waste of my time to go out there at all. But that's a lesson learned."

"Just how angry was Simon when you told him that it would have to be repaired for the same problem again?" Tessa pursed her lips.

"He was pretty angry." Dean rubbed the back of his neck.

"Do you think he was angry enough to kill Richard?" Tessa asked.

Cassie froze as Tessa's words hung in the air between them.

"No idea. Look, I don't want to get involved in any of it." Dean took a step back.

"Just a second." Tessa held up her hands. "With your help, the police might be able to catch

Richard's killer before they have a chance to hurt someone else. Anything you can tell us might be helpful."

"If you really want to know who might have had it in for Richard that bad, I can tell you a lot of people did." Dean wrung his bandana between his hands again.

"Like who?" Tessa's tone softened.

"No one specific. Everyone who came to me from Richard wanted to know why I charge so much more than him. Of course I let them know Richard's work is shoddy and he's slimy and is always undercutting me. But there is one person who I could single out, I guess. But you need to keep my name out of it."

"Of course. Who was it?" Tessa asked.

"Lewis, a farmer from Little Leaf Creek. Apparently, Richard sold his stolen horse trailer back to him. He kept pushing me to try and help him prove it was his. He wanted to prove what Richard could be doing and if I was involved in it. I told him I had nothing to do with it, and there was no way I could prove it was his, and unless he was going to get something fixed he'd have to move on because I had plenty of work to do. He said he understood and he'd be calling me soon. I don't know why he would be calling me soon. Maybe it had something to do with trying to catch Richard."

"Did you try and do something about Richard undercutting you? Maybe try to prove his work was shoddy or he was dishonest? It was hurting your business, wasn't it? I would think you would want to put a stop to it, wouldn't you?" Tessa asked.

"I think you shouldn't try to assume much about what I would do. I know better than to go against the son of someone who was so revered. I just had to be satisfied with taking the people who got fed up with Richard, and I knew they all eventually would. If he'd continued to do that kind of work on everyone's equipment that he did on Simon's, people would wise up to it eventually."

"You would hope so." Tessa nodded.

"I need to get back to work." Dean turned around and walked farther back into the shop.

Tessa started toward the jeep. "Let's roll. I doubt we'll find out much from Lewis, so I want to go to the bakery. Try to find out if whoever was making deliveries around the time of the murder saw something."

"Sounds good. But I don't think it will still be open. It's getting late." Cassie joined her in the jeep.

"True." Tessa glanced at her watch. "It probably opens early and closes early."

"Let's see." Cassie typed on her phone and nodded. "I think this must be the place. It's already closed. It opens at seven. I have a shift at the diner, late morning, so why don't we go there first thing."

"Good idea." Tessa headed toward home.

CHAPTER 8

The following morning, Cassie woke from a fitful night's sleep to the smell of coffee. When she'd gotten home the previous evening Sebastian had been on his farm working. She'd started reading in bed and planned to wait up for him, but after just a few pages she'd drifted off to sleep and awoke briefly when he got into bed. She quickly got ready, then walked into the kitchen as Sebastian turned to face her.

"Morning, beautiful." Sebastian put down his vegetable drink and opened his arms to her. His charming smile and warm Southern accent always took her breath away.

"Morning." Cassie felt his strong arms wrap around her.

"Sorry I didn't see you yesterday. I wanted to speak to you properly about what happened, but everything got away from me."

"I missed you. Tessa and I did a little sleuthing."

"Of course you did. You're always so curious." Sebastian handed her a coffee.

"Thank you. What do you know about Richard?"

"Honestly, Cassie, not a lot. I have to say I did my best to avoid him. There's always been some kind of ill feelings floating around town about him. He had a reputation for cutting corners and making a quick buck, even when he worked with his dad. And I can repair my own equipment. I didn't need his help. But I've heard plenty of stories from others about him."

"What kind of stories?" Cassie had a sip of coffee.

"Oh, just that he undercut people. Did a lousy job. Things like that."

"Anyone in particular have it in for him?"

"Not that I know of." Sebastian hesitated and averted his gaze.

"You don't sound convinced. I know you have a lot of history with the locals. Maybe there's something you don't want to tell me because it makes you uncomfortable? Or are you protecting someone?"

"Look, if I thought it was important to the investigation I'd tell you, but I worry it would point the finger at the wrong person. And I don't want it getting back to Tessa and Ollie. Trust me, my friend had nothing to do with Richard's murder, okay?"

"Okay." Cassie wanted to try to get him to give her more information, but she had to trust his judgment.

"I have to head out. I'll catch up with you later." Sebastian wrapped his arms around her and gave her a long kiss.

"Love you." Cassie pulled back from him.

"Love you, too." Sebastian walked over to the front door and swung it open.

Tessa stood there with her hand poised, ready to knock. "Good timing."

"I was just on my way out." Sebastian held the door for her, then continued out onto the porch.

"Well, he was in a hurry," Tessa said.

"He was. It sounds like he knows someone who might have had something against Richard, but he doesn't want to point a finger at them."

"Interesting. I hope he reveals whatever he knows, soon. Every lead needs to be investigated. I know you wanted waffles, but I thought we could grab something at the bakery. I'll make them for you tomorrow?"

"Sounds perfect." Cassie followed Tessa out to the jeep. "You know, I've been thinking, we believe the person who killed Richard was livid. Dean didn't seem to be that angry about Richard stealing his customers."

"Anyone can snap. Actually, I think his calmness might make him a little more suspicious." Tessa pulled onto the highway that led to Rombsby. "He should have been angry. Furious even. But instead he just acted a little annoyed. Don't you find that odd? He must be desperate for money because apparently Richard was always taking his customers by undercutting him."

"Well, he does work at the auto repair shop, too. But you're right, it does seem strange he wasn't angrier. But maybe he's more relaxed about it now that Richard is dead. It's helped solve his problems. The competition is dead. I'll make a note of that." Cassie jotted down the note beside his name. "And, also, his shirt was torn. That's something to consider. Didn't Ollie find a piece of cloth by Gerry's hoof at the crime scene?"

"Yes, he did. It was dirty, but from what I could

see, it looked dark, maybe blue or green or even black. It could have come from Dean's T-shirt. My theory is, and it's just a theory at the moment, that whoever killed Richard had their shirt torn somehow, or maybe their pants. It's a long shot, honestly. That material may not even be related to the case. Here we are. We'll talk about it more after." Tessa parked in front of a small bakery.

"This place is cute." Cassie stepped out of the jeep and looked at the wooden door and hand-painted sign above it. Rombsby Bakery. "Has it been here long?"

"No, not long at all. I've driven past it but never been in." Tessa followed Cassie toward the door.

Cassie opened it and held it for Tessa. The aroma of freshly baked bread immediately hit Cassie and made her stomach rumble.

A woman who looked to be about thirty, with an apron on and her long black hair tied in a ponytail, looked up as they walked toward the counter. Her name tag read Haley. "Good morning. What can I get for you?"

"Morning." Tessa's eyes widened as she studied the selection. "An apple-cinnamon muffin, please." She walked over to the self-serve coffee station and began preparing their coffees in two to-go cups.

"Everything looks so delicious." Cassie looked over the display. "I'll get the same."

"Coming right up." Haley picked up a pair of tongs.

"I heard you deliver to Little Leaf Creek?" Tessa kept her voice friendly as she glanced over at Haley.

"Sure do." Haley smiled. "It's a new service we offer. We were just trying it out, but it's had such a good response, I think we'll keep it going."

"Oh, that's a great idea. Did you deliver to Sheila's and Simon's farms yesterday morning? On Old Creek Road?" Tessa handed Cassie a coffee cup.

"Thank you." Cassie had only a few sips of her coffee at home, so she was ready for another.

"Yes, I did. Well, I mean the bakery did. Clay took it out there." Haley put their muffins in paper bags.

"Is it possible to speak to him for a minute, please?" Tessa asked.

"What about?" Haley handed Tessa a muffin.

"Thank you." Tessa gave her some cash to pay for their order. "Someone was found dead on Simon's farm."

"I heard about that. But why do you want to

speak to Clay about it?" Haley looked between them.

"We just want to know if he noticed anything when he was out there. That's all." Tessa had a bite of the muffin. "Oh, this is delicious."

"Thank you. They're one of our best sellers. Clay is the baker and the delivery man." Haley turned around and called into the back. "Clay, some customers want to talk to you."

"Give me a minute," a deep voice drifted out.

A couple of minutes later, a tall and burly man, who looked to be about fifty, with a bald head and a rotund stomach, walked into the front of the bakery.

"Clay." Tessa recognized him. He used to work at the coffee shop in Little Leaf Creek. He'd moved after his wife had died in a car accident.

"Tessa, what are you doing here? I haven't seen you in ages." Clay smiled.

"I wanted to try out the new bakery and get some information. I didn't know you worked here," Tessa said.

"I own it, with Haley." Clay glanced over at Haley.

"I just want to grab some more milk." Haley started toward the kitchen.

"Okay." Clay walked closer to the counter.

"You delivered to Simon's and Sheila's farms, yesterday morning?" Tessa asked.

"Yes. Before poor Richard was found dead." Clay grimaced. "Are you working for the police again? I thought you were retired."

"I am retired, but we were out there at Sheila's yesterday, and we want to see if maybe we can help get to the bottom of this. The quicker this is solved, the better for everyone. We just wanted to check if you noticed anything out of the ordinary? Anything out of place when you made the delivery? Did you see Richard or anyone else?" Tessa held up her muffin. "The muffins are delicious, by the way."

"Thank you. That's a huge compliment coming from you." Clay smiled. "Tessa, the great baker. And no, I didn't notice anything. I've been thinking about it since I heard. To be honest, I was a bit distracted."

"You were?" Tessa asked.

"Yes, I almost had an accident as I turned into Old Creek Road," Clay huffed. "Someone pulled out right in front of me. Their car was bright pink, so you couldn't miss it. But I was lucky to avoid hitting them. They were driving so fast."

"Did you notice anything about the vehicle, or anything else?" Tessa had a sip of coffee.

"No, nothing." Clay clutched his chest with his hand. "Gave me the fright of my life."

"I'm sure. Has Ollie spoken to you, yet?" Tessa asked.

"He did. I told him exactly what I told you." Clay picked up a pair of tongs and straightened some donuts.

"Okay," Tessa said as a beeping sound came from the kitchen.

"I have to take the bread rolls out. It was good to see you, Tessa. Sorry I couldn't be more help." Clay walked into the back. "Haley, please watch the front."

Before Tessa could say a word, Cassie lunged behind the counter and quickly flipped through some papers that hung on a hook on the wall on a clipboard and snapped a few photos.

"Cassie!" Tessa hissed at her under her breath. "Get out of there. Quick."

Cassie heard footsteps heading toward them from the kitchen as she rounded the counter and hurried toward the door.

CHAPTER 9

"That was close." Tessa followed Cassie out to the jeep.

"I know, I'm sorry." Cassie hopped into the passenger seat.

"What are the photos of?"

"The delivery schedule and acknowledgment of receipt." Cassie scanned through the pictures. "According to this, Clay delivers to Sheila, then Simon. And it looks like Sheila signed for her delivery that morning, but there's nothing next to Simon's name, so maybe no one was around to sign for the delivery."

"So, maybe Clay saw Richard on Simon's farm when he delivered to Sheila. Just like we could see the field, maybe he also could," Tessa suggested.

"That's very possible. Then when he made the delivery to Simon and saw no one was around, he took the opportunity to kill Richard."

"Or he just wanted to speak and things got out of hand."

"But why? What could his motive be?" Cassie asked.

"No idea. It's probably a dead end." Tessa stopped at a red light. "You know Clay moved to Rombsby from Little Leaf Creek when his wife died in a car accident?"

"That's terrible." Cassie's heart lurched. The memories of her late husband being killed in a crash came flooding back.

"It was such a tragedy. She was only thirty-six. I'll get Mark to look into him. We know he was in the area around the time of the murder. That's enough to dig into him more." Tessa turned onto the main road. "We'll go talk to Mark now."

"Okay." Cassie looked over her notes.

Tessa turned into the parking lot of Mark's office building. "Let's go see what Mark's turned up." She stepped out of the jeep and heard Cassie follow her. She could predict her next words.

"Oh, yes, I can't wait to see Mark, either." Cassie teased as she caught up to her.

"You know that's a bit of a broken record." Tessa gave her a nudge with her elbow. "He's just our best resource at the moment."

"Is that what the kids are calling it these days?" Cassie grinned. "Best resource?"

"I don't even know what that's supposed to mean. Shush. We need to be serious about all this or he won't be serious. You know that man wastes so much time joking around."

"Trying to get you to smile." Cassie started up the stairs beside Tessa.

"Acting ridiculous."

"Trying to get you to laugh."

"Behaving like a childish fool," Tessa huffed.

"Trying to get you to kiss him." Cassie laughed as they reached the top of the stairs.

"Cassie!" Tessa snapped her fingers as she stalked past her. "Not a word of that!"

"He obviously cares about you a lot. I mean, the evidence is there." Cassie ducked as Tessa swung a glare over her shoulder.

"What evidence?" Mark startled them both as he leaned against the doorway of his office. "I heard you two coming." He enveloped Tessa in a quick hug, then pulled back and met her eyes.

"Uh, evidence that Cassie almost got us caught photographing," Tessa muttered.

"Tessa," Cassie gasped.

"Sounds like an interesting story." Mark smoothed down his wide tie which featured piano keys in several different vibrant colors.

"It will have to wait. There's more pressing matters. Can you see if you can find out if Clay Donaldson might have had a motive to kill Richard? It's a long shot, but he was delivering goods from Rombsby Bakery to the farms around the time of the murder." Tessa followed him into his office. "But first, can you see if you can turn something up about someone who might be peddling stolen farm equipment?"

"I can help you with that, but only if you promise me you're not going to ask me how. Not now and not later," Mark said.

"I'll let you have your secrets. I just hope they're nothing that can get you into trouble." Tessa grinned as he reached for her hand and squeezed it.

"Now, Tessa, I'm always in trouble, but I always find my way out. Sometimes with a little help from you, right?" Mark looked at her a moment longer.

Tessa couldn't resist a smile.

"Give me a few minutes and let me see what I

can come up with." Mark stepped into the inner office and closed the door behind him.

"Must be top secret." Cassie raised her eyebrows.

"He has his ways. I think it's better he keeps me in the dark about them," Tessa said.

"Seems to me like he'd do just about anything to impress you." Cassie smiled.

"He's just invested in making sure there isn't a murderer running loose around town." Tessa settled in one of the vinyl cushioned chairs near a window in the office.

"Do you think we should update Ollie?" Cassie scrolled through her phone.

"Let's just wait and see what Mark can come up with. Hopefully, it's something that will point us in the right direction. If Richard really was buying stolen equipment, that definitely could be a connection to his murderer. In my experience criminals are criminals, and many can easily become murderers when pushed hard enough."

"So, maybe Richard decided to stop buying the stolen equipment and it caused the seller to be angry—just one possibility. Another one might be that Richard really didn't know he was buying stolen merchandise, and when he found out that he'd sold

Lewis his own stolen trailer, Richard confronted whoever he bought it from and that person decided that he had to go, so that he couldn't tell anyone where he purchased it."

"It's also possible that Richard was legitimate, and someone else was sabotaging the equipment and whoever it was killed him to keep him quiet. It still surprises me that they would do it on Simon's farm, though." Tessa took a deep breath. "If we clue Ollie in now, he might jump the gun and spook whoever was dealing in the stolen equipment. He has all those rules and regulations he has to follow, whereas we have a lot more room to navigate."

Cassie's phone began ringing. She held it up to show Tessa Ollie's name on the display.

CHAPTER 10

"Hi, Ollie. I'll put you on speaker. Tessa is also here." Cassie pressed the speakerphone button.

"Good, I need to speak with both of you." Oliver's authoritative voice filled the room.

"I'm here." Tessa stood up and walked closer to the phone. "Are you onto something?"

"Only the two of you. You've been interviewing all of my potential suspects."

"We just had a few chats." Tessa glanced at Cassie.

"I shouldn't be surprised. I know." Oliver's voice held a hint of tension. "Is there anything you'd like to share with me?"

"Tessa!" Mark's voice boomed from inside his

office just before he stepped out. "You owe me a kiss, you gorgeous goddess. I found exactly who you're looking for!"

Tessa gestured wildly for Cassie to turn off the speakerphone.

Cassie fumbled with her phone but couldn't reach the button before Oliver spoke up again.

"So, you're with Mark?" Oliver's voice drifted through the phone.

Mark froze in the doorway of his office and stared at the phone. "Is that Oliver? Did he just hear me call you a gorgeous goddess?"

"Let's just get back to the subject at hand." Tessa cleared her throat. "Mark, why don't you just tell all of us what you found?"

"Tessa." Mark hesitated as he glanced from the phone to her. "I'm not sure I'm comfortable with that."

"Anything you can tell her you should be able to tell me. Or maybe I need to come there in person?" Oliver's tone grew stern.

"Ollie, relax." Cassie looked over at Tessa. "Whatever it is, we'd tell you either way."

"It's okay, I'll tell you." Mark stepped closer to the phone. "Tessa and Cassie asked me to find a local dealer of stolen farm equipment."

"I've been barking up that tree, too, but I haven't been able to find anyone. No one's talking." Oliver sighed.

"My source has given me a name. It's Kirk Parkers. He's lived in the area for a few years but doesn't have any family around here and stays on the outskirts of Rombsby." Mark glanced up at Tessa. "I'll give Tessa the contact information I have for him."

"Who's your source?" Oliver's disembodied voice still managed to be commanding as he spoke to Mark.

"I can't tell you that, Ollie." Mark shook his head. "Either take the information or don't, but that's as much as I can do for you."

"I don't have to ask, Mark. I can get a court order."

"Oliver!" Tessa's own tone reflected Oliver's commanding voice.

"Tessa, this is a murder investigation. You can't expect me to treat him differently from anyone else," Oliver said.

"You can get whatever you want, Ollie. Feel free." Mark sighed. "It's not going to change anything. Instead of wasting your time on all that paperwork, why don't you try tracking down the lead?"

"Why don't you try not telling me how to do my job?" Oliver snapped.

"Okay, okay." Cassie took the phone off speaker and put it up to her ear. "You're breaking up, Ollie. It must be a bad connection." Her cheeks reddened as she ended the call.

"Nice one, Cassie." Mark smiled.

"He's not going to like that." Tessa cringed.

"We shared the information with him that he needs. What he does with it is his choice." Cassie passed a worried look in Mark's direction. "But what if he does show up here with a court order or handcuffs?"

"Don't worry. Ollie knows I'm a good resource. He's just a little sore because he caught Tessa and me out to dinner the other night. I get it. She's like a mother to him. It's going to take him some time to get used to the idea of seeing us together. Even though he says he's supportive of our relationship, and he and Mirabel had me over for Christmas and everything, he's protective of her." Mark draped his arm around Tessa's shoulders. "Having Mirabel trying to get him to relax about it is a positive. He'll get used to it. I promise."

"You have no idea how stubborn that boy is," Tessa groaned.

"I think I might." Mark laughed. "I think I know who he gets it from." He winked at her.

"We should get going if we're going to go talk to Kirk. I'm supposed to be at the diner for my shift soon." Cassie double-checked the time on her watch.

"And we need to beat Ollie to him. I'm sure he's organizing to get over there as we speak. I don't think he has the address, so it might take him a while," Tessa said.

"All right, if the two of you are going to go talk to Kirk, you're going to need some extra equipment." Mark slid a painting, hanging behind his receptionist's desk, to the side and revealed a small safe. He punched a few keys on the keypad, then opened the safe. As he reached inside, Tessa cleared her throat.

"Don't show me anything in there you can't legally have, Mark."

"Would I ever?" Mark gasped as he pulled out a pouch about the size of his palm. "This is just a little something I keep around for those clients I have to pay home visits to, whose pets aren't terribly friendly. Kirk is known for having guard dogs. I don't know if it's just rumors, but you can never be too prepared." He tossed her the pouch.

Tessa opened the pouch and peered inside. "What are these? Treats?"

"Delicious treats. They'll distract the dogs. Trust me. Take them with you. You might need them. I only keep them in the safe because I have a client who visits me with her therapy dog and he always finds the treats if I leave them out. He's very well trained, but he has a big appetite." Mark walked them both to the door. "If you don't have to use them, give them to Harry. But tell him they're from me."

"Okay," Tessa laughed. Mark was well known to butter up Harry with a few treats. But he usually snuck them to him from his plate, under the table. "Let me know if you find out anything else."

"I will." Mark smiled, then pulled her into a hug. "Be careful. I know you can handle yourself, but Kirk can be a slippery guy."

"Don't worry, we'll get the truth out of him." Tessa nodded to Cassie as she passed her and continued down the stairs.

Cassie followed after her, wishing she felt the same confidence that Tessa did.

CHAPTER 11

"It's been a wild couple of days, hasn't it?" Tessa turned onto a narrow side road that soon became an even narrower dirt road.

"It certainly has. Hopefully, I can get some information at the diner. I'm sure everyone in town will be gathered together gossiping about the murder. If I listen in to their conversations, I just might get us a new lead." Cassie squinted at the dilapidated house they rolled up to. "Are you sure this is the right place?"

"It's the address Mark gave me." Tessa shifted the jeep into park. "Let's have a look around." She stepped out onto the dirt driveway.

"Is that him there?" Cassie gasped as she watched a man get into an old pickup truck.

A second later, the truck roared to life. Two dogs that looked like Maltese terriers barked through the open window of the passenger seat as the truck zipped across the field and disappeared down the street.

"Well, they didn't look like guard dogs." Tessa laughed.

"No, they certainly didn't. He must have seen us coming. We'll never catch up with him now."

"Maybe we don't have to. The fact he took off running like that is pretty damning. Don't you think?"

"Maybe. But as you would say, it's not evidence." Cassie looked over the small house. "This thing looks like it hasn't been touched in years. If he's the thief, he might not be making much money off his criminal ways."

"It may not look like much, but the property value of this place is pretty high." Tessa walked up to the front door and nudged it with her toe. When it didn't budge she tried the doorknob. "It's closed and locked."

"If he'd left it open we might have been able to take a peek inside." Cassie cupped her hands around her eyes and peered through the thick glass window.

"Let's have a look around a bit." Tessa walked

over to the barn with Cassie a few steps behind her. She started to step inside but froze at the entrance.

"What is it? Do you see something?"

"I'd say so." Tessa turned on the flashlight on her phone and pointed the beam of light at a pile of crumpled clothes just inside the barn door. "Does that look like blood to you?"

"It sure does."

"We definitely found something." Tessa glanced at the time on her phone, then looked up at Cassie. "It's almost time for your shift."

"You're right, but we can't leave this here. It needs to be taken into evidence. I'll just be a little late."

"You go on, take the jeep." Tessa placed the keys in her hand. "I'll get a ride with Ollie. He's going to want to see this."

"Thank you." Cassie hurried over to the jeep and waved to Tessa as she drove away.

On the short drive to the diner, Cassie thought about the possibility of Kirk being the murderer. If Kirk had killed Richard, why would he leave his bloodstained clothes right by the barn door? Wouldn't he have gotten rid of them? If he made money from dealing in stolen equipment, why was he living on a run-down property? Certainly, if

Richard had threatened to go to the police, Kirk would have had reason to kill him. But why do it on Simon's property with a chance of there being witnesses nearby?

Cassie parked in front of the diner and headed to the door. As she predicted, just about every table and booth was packed full of locals. The roar of the various conversations filled the air, but they all had the same theme. She was welcomed by Mirabel's bright smile as she hurried an order over to a booth. Before Cassie had a chance to say a proper hello to Mirabel or the other waitress, Tamera, she already had an order to place with the kitchen. She had wanted to ask Mirabel if she'd heard anything about the murder but she hadn't had a chance as shortly after Cassie's shift started, Mirabel had run out the door to go watch Maisy's basketball game. Mirabel had become the guardian of the young teen when her grandmother couldn't take care of her anymore.

What felt like minutes later had actually been hours. Cassie hurried toward a table with two burgers and french fries for a couple of men who she recognized as local farmers and Sebastian's friends. She set down their plates in front of them as their conversation continued to flow around her.

"Like I said, he's the luckiest guy in the world,

right?" Joey's thick eyebrows hiked upward along the long plane of his forehead. "Everyone else around here is being hit with a streak of bad luck. Equipment failures, supply issues, even equipment being stolen. But this guy, he's just chugging along like nothing can stop him. He's got all of that expensive equipment, and it hasn't been touched. It just doesn't make sense." He took a long swig of his iced tea, then set the glass down hard on the table. Liquid sloshed over the rim and splashed across his rough hand, but he didn't seem to notice. "You tell me, Lon, how does all of the bad luck miss him?"

"I don't know, but I think it probably has to do with all that money he has." The skinnier man sank down in his chair as a sly smile crossed his lips. "It's hard to have bad luck when you're in a billion-dollar corporation's pocket, right?"

"Yeah, I suppose." Joey glanced up at Cassie, startled. "Sorry, Cassie, I didn't even see you there. Thanks for the grub."

"No problem. You seemed pretty focused on your conversation." Cassie lowered her voice. "I can't help but wonder who you're talking about."

"A guy named Brent, Brent Davies. He's quite new around here, but he doesn't seem to be having any of the trouble we are. What about Sebastian?

Has anything been happening on his farm?" Joey had a french fry.

"No, luckily. But he did just go over to his friend Phil's place to help him fix his four-wheeler. He's helped out a few neighbors actually. Like he always does. Any idea who might be causing all of these problems?" Cassie's thoughts shifted back to Dean, and the man who'd taken off before she'd even had the chance to talk to him.

"I wish I knew. I can promise you, if I did, he wouldn't be around long." Joey snapped his thick thumb and middle finger together as his lip curled into a sneer. "He's messing with people's livelihoods. He's bound to get payback soon enough."

"Like Richard did?" Cassie regretted the question the moment his eyes narrowed.

"Why would you say something like that, Cassie? Do you know something about what happened to Richard?"

"Yeah, tell us." Lon leaned closer to her. "I know you're tight with Ollie. What's the inside word on Richard's murder?"

"Sorry to disappoint you, but I really don't know. What I do know is that, of course, Ollie is working hard to make sure Richard's killer is brought to justice. I just asked because I've heard some rumors Richard had been upsetting some people around here. Do you know anything about that?" Cassie looked between them.

"I haven't heard anything like that, but if I did, I'd be smart enough to keep it to myself." Joey pointed past her. "Looks like someone needs you over there, Cassie."

Cassie caught sight of Sebastian in the doorway of the diner. She glanced back at the two men and flashed them a smile, then walked over to Sebastian.

CHAPTER 12

"What are you doing here?" Cassie gave Sebastian a tight hug.

"Good to see you, too." Sebastian smiled.

"You have no idea how good."

"Your shift is just about over, right? I thought I'd give you a ride home." Sebastian met her eyes. "You can give me an update on what's happening."

"I already settled everything up. I was just delivering some meals for Tamera. But actually, I drove Tessa's jeep here, so I'll have to drop it at her place." Cassie hesitated, then lowered her voice. "But maybe you can give me some information about a local farmer?"

"Sure, anything I can do to help." Sebastian pulled back as Tessa walked up to them.

"Brent Davies, do you know him?" Cassie asked.

Sebastian cringed, then nodded. "Yes, I know him."

"Great, then you can give us his address and some background information." Tessa smiled. "Mark let me know he's someone we should speak to."

"If you're going to go speak with him, I'll go with you." Sebastian held up one hand before Cassie could begin protesting. "I know you and Tessa can handle yourselves, but I'm curious about this guy. I keep hearing so many rumors. I've been meaning to go have a look at what he's done to his farm and welcome him to the area. This is the perfect excuse."

"I'm not sure how welcoming we'll be." Tessa gestured for him to follow her out the door to her jeep. "But it never hurts to have you along. Those good looks get you everywhere."

"I think that's a compliment?" Sebastian climbed into the back of the jeep.

"It's definitely a compliment." Cassie hopped into the passenger seat. "The fact alone that Tessa is letting you come along is a huge compliment."

"Letting me?" Sebastian raised his eyebrows as he leaned forward from the back seat. "I see now what it must have been like for Ollie."

"Hush back there, or I'll leave you on the sidewalk," Tessa mumbled as she started the jeep. She glanced over at Cassie with a sparkle in her eyes but a scowl on her face. "He'd better behave himself, or we're going to make sure he has to find a different ride home."

"Don't worry." Cassie winked over her shoulder at Sebastian. "He has impeccable manners to go along with those good looks."

"That's it, then?" Sebastian's eyes widened as Tessa's foot on the gas propelled him back against his seat. "You just want me to talk nice and look pretty?"

"Someone has to do it." Tessa took a hard right turn. "Cassie deserves a break now and then."

"Aw, how sweet." Cassie grinned. "What's the hurry, Tessa?"

"I just want to get there as soon as possible, so we can have a look around." Tessa gunned the engine again.

"A look around?" Sebastian leaned forward. "What exactly is the plan here? We're just making a friendly visit, right? Not conducting a full search of the property?"

"We're going to do whatever we think we can get away with." Tessa slammed on the brakes and turned onto a nearly hidden side road. "Hang on, that road jumped out at me."

Cassie gripped the dashboard.

"There we go, see? We're already here." Tessa pointed in front of her.

Cassie took a sharp breath, both from the wild driving, and the sudden appearance of the farm that sprawled out before her. Compared to most homes in the area, the farmhouse looked more like a mansion with three stories and several outbuildings. One of the barns had been built and decorated to look just like the farmhouse. "Wow. I don't think I've ever seen a farm as nice as this."

"Ouch?" Sebastian followed her out of the jeep. "My farm is decent."

"Sure, but it's modest." Cassie cleared her throat. "I mean, I don't think I've seen one as fancy. Most farmers don't go all out with these decorative fences and splashy paint colors."

"I see." Sebastian nodded as he slid his hands into the pockets of his jeans. "Well, it's a lot easier to do when you have the kind of financial backing this place does."

"Look, there's someone on the porch." Tessa strode toward the wide wraparound porch as a tall and burly man neared the edge of it.

"Wow, visitors." He offered his hand to them. "I wasn't expecting anyone. I haven't really had any visitors since I moved here. People haven't been that welcoming."

"This is Tessa and Cassie, and I'm Sebastian." Sebastian took his hand in a firm shake, then released it as he smiled. "It can take people a little while to warm up, but once they do, you'll be part of us. You're stuck."

"Brent. But I guess you already knew that. Something tells me you're not here to bring me muffins or a welcome basket." Brent's gaze settled on Sebastian. "I've heard a lot about you, but I'm not sure if I should believe all of those stories about what a good neighbor you are, when you haven't even bothered to show up and say hello."

"I'm sorry about that. I've been a little busy." Sebastian shrugged as he glanced away from him.

"Oh?" Brent narrowed his eyes. "It has nothing to do with the fact that I have corporate backing for my farm? I know that's not a popular thing around here."

"Not at all. There's just been a lot going on lately," Sebastian said.

"Yes, he's right." Cassie slung her arm around his shoulders. "We got married, then we were away for our honeymoon, and we've been busy setting up a home together, getting everything arranged, and all of that."

"We're not only here to welcome you" Tessa took a step toward Brent. "We also have some questions for you, and we're hoping you'll be kind enough to answer them."

"Well then, the truth comes out." Brent shrugged. "After this warm welcome, how could I not? What do you want to ask me about?"

"A man was murdered yesterday morning, on a farm not too far from here." Tessa squinted at him. "Did you hear about that?"

"Yeah, I've heard something about that." Brent crossed his arms. "I really thought moving to this town would be different than living in the big city, but now I'm starting to wonder if it's any safer here than it was there."

"A good number of things have been happening around here lately that make it seem a lot less safe. Like farm equipment being stolen or vandalized, and supplies disappearing, but from what I've been told, you haven't really experienced any of that," Cassie said.

Brent's gaze passed over Cassie and settled on Sebastian. "So, instead of coming here to welcome me, as a good neighbor would, you've come here to question my good fortune?"

"Not everyone has a backup plan. If their farm fails, they'll lose everything. So, what may seem like little inconveniences to you are huge blows for them. It's just odd that you haven't had any of the same bad luck." Sebastian squared his shoulders. "And you're right, I should have made more of an effort to come over and introduce myself. But I knew the man who owned the farm before you, who was run out of his home, who sacrificed everything to try to save it, only to lose it in the end."

"I'm sure he was paid well." Brent's lips formed a tight, straight line.

"There isn't enough money in the world." Sebastian shook his head.

"We're not here to debate values. We're here to find out if there's some reason why you've been immune to these attacks. Is there anything you might be able to share with us?" Tessa asked. "Maybe you've been hit with some of the incidents but you've been reluctant to report it? Not everyone wants to get the police involved. I understand that."

"Does this town have police?" Brent chuckled. "I'm sure they're dusting off their boots right now wondering how to solve a murder."

"Is that supposed to offend me?" Tessa pointed at herself. "It doesn't. Are you going to answer the question?"

"All right. No, I haven't had any trouble." Brent smirked as he looked between them. "That's because big-city life teaches you one thing farm life never can. That's street smarts. When I heard about all of the crime going on, I decided to take matters into my own hands."

"What do you mean by that?" Sebastian asked.

"I mean, I paid the criminal off." Brent gestured to the bottom step of his porch. "I left a bundle of cash with a note that told him if he'd leave my property and possessions alone, I'd keep the money coming."

"Are you saying you leave money out for the person vandalizing the farms in this community, so yours doesn't get touched?" Sebastian's tone hardened. "Is that really what you thought was the best solution?"

"Whoa there." Brent held up his hands. "Like I said, I'll do things my way. It worked."

"It worked, but you're also providing funds to this criminal to continue to harass the farmers around here who can't afford to leave out a bundle of cash. You're encouraging behavior that's going to lead to the destruction of this entire area!" Sebastian gestured around him.

"All right, I think he's answered enough of our questions. We can let Ollie sort this out from here." Cassie wasn't surprised that Sebastian was annoyed with Brent.

"Ollie? That fellow that walks around this town with a badge on his chest?" Brent pointed at his chest. "Sure, send him on by. I'll leave a bundle of cash out for him, too."

CHAPTER 13

"Ollie would never take a bribe from anyone!" Tessa pursed her lips.

"If you say so." Brent looked at each of them. "I'm not trying to cause any trouble. You asked me a question, I answered it. I'm not going to put my farm or my possessions at risk for anyone."

"You do realize that encouraging this criminal is going to put the whole area at a huge risk?" Sebastian raised his eyebrows. "You have a responsibility to your neighbors."

"To which neighbors? The ones who haven't bothered to welcome me? The ones who have been bad-mouthing me this whole time?" Brent shook his head. "No, I don't have any responsibility to anyone but me."

"And the corporation that owns you," Sebastian said.

"What are you going to do about it?" Brent smirked.

"Look, just calm down." Cassie patted the air. "We came here for your help."

"You came here to accuse me of something." Brent put his hands on his hips.

"And we were right to." Tessa crossed her arms. "You've been bribing a criminal. I think you should give us some information before I report this to the police."

"Wait just a second." Brent focused his attention on Tessa. "I haven't done anything wrong. I just left money out on my porch, and in the morning it was gone."

"You didn't just leave money. You left a note. It's bribery," Tessa snapped.

"You'll never be able to prove it." Brent crossed his arms.

"And you didn't catch who it was? Didn't get a name? Or a look at their face?" Sebastian pointed to the camera positioned by Brent's front door. "I doubt that he didn't show up on there."

"Oh, that thing?" Brent cleared his throat. "It's just for show. I don't have it hooked up. I don't want my every move being recorded. You have no idea who can access that. But it works as a great deterrent."

"And it also makes me doubt your story. Why would this criminal risk walking in front of that camera?" Tessa glanced at the camera. "I think you know exactly who's behind the destruction that's happening on the farms around here. The fact that you would lie to us about that makes me wonder what else you would lie to us about."

"I have nothing to lie about. I'm an honest businessman, just trying to keep my business going." Brent took a step back from Tessa's scrutinizing gaze.

"Honest, huh?" Tessa gave a short laugh. "If you were honest, you wouldn't be helping a criminal or hiding his identity. I don't for a second believe you've been leaving money out for a random person. You must know who it is."

"Like I said, I don't have to tell you anything." Brent ascended the steps and backed up farther on the porch. "You're making up stories."

"Are we?" Sebastian pointed at a toolbox pushed back against the house with a half-torn towel strewn across it. "Something tells me that's not your toolbox. It looks well used, and I don't see a single thing around here that doesn't look brand new."

"Grasping at straws. What do you want to do? Inspect the toolbox?" Brent laughed.

"Can we?" Cassie eyed the dark green towel on top of it. "You say you had nothing to do with any of this. So, you shouldn't mind if we have a look."

"I didn't have anything to do with it. But I do mind if you continue to snoop on my property. In fact, I think it's time for all of you to leave." Brent pointed toward the street. "I know it wouldn't do any good to call the police, since you have them in your back pocket, but I have other ways of making you go."

"Oh?" Tessa raised her eyebrows. "Are you threatening us?"

"If you don't leave, I just might be." Brent snatched up the toolbox, along with the towel, and stormed back into his house. As the door slammed shut behind him, Tessa started up the steps.

"What's the plan, Tessa?" Cassie followed after her. "Are you going to bang the door down?"

"Cassie. He can't get away with what he's doing." Tessa walked up to the door, then froze.

"She's right, Cassie. He's ruining lives by

encouraging that thief. He has to be stopped!" Sebastian joined them on the porch.

"I know he does." Cassie looked at him. "But certainly not like this. We aren't going to achieve anything by making him angrier."

"Cassie's right. We aren't going to achieve anything here. We need to follow the proper steps to get Brent investigated." Tessa took a deep breath, then turned around to face them both. "It's no use getting upset. That's not how crimes are solved."

"I know, but I can't believe he did that." Sebastian descended the steps to the driveway.

"I just wish the trip out here had yielded us a little more information." Tessa opened the door to the jeep.

"I'd say knowing he's bribing the thief is pretty good information." Sebastian climbed into the back seat.

Tessa started the jeep, but before she could put it in drive her cell phone began ringing. She reached into her purse and pulled it out. "Cassie, see who it is, please." She tossed it over to her as she started backing out of the driveway.

Cassie caught the phone and checked the screen. "It's Mark."

Tessa stopped and put the jeep back into park.

"Maybe he's found something new." She took the phone back and answered it. "Hi, Mark, do you have something for me?" She took a sharp breath, then nodded. "All right, thanks so much. We'll head right over."

"What is it?" Cassie asked as Tessa ended the call.

"Mark just received an update on the police scanner. It sounds like Ollie has our runner Kirk in custody. Mark confirmed it with his source." Tessa shifted the jeep back into reverse. "It's time we paid Ollie a visit. I want to know for sure if he has him in custody and what he plans to do with him."

Cassie recalled seeing the clothes with red stains on them. If Kirk did turn out to be the killer, she was relieved they hadn't had a chance to interact with him.

CHAPTER 14

After dropping off Sebastian at the diner so he could pick up his truck, Cassie and Tessa headed to the police station.

Cassie pushed open the door of the bustling station. She watched as officers rushed past her in different directions. "It's a little wild in here." She held the door open for Tessa.

"It is. They might have the murderer in custody. That's a fantastic feeling." Tessa's voice rose with excitement. After getting the go-ahead from the officer at the front desk, she made her way toward Oliver's office.

"How?" Oliver looked up at them as they walked inside. "I was just about to call you, and somehow you're already here."

"We came right over when we heard you caught Kirk. Sorry we didn't stop for champagne. I'll get you some later." Tessa smiled.

"You might want to hold off on the champagne." Oliver looked from her to Cassie, then back again. "How did you know we caught him?"

"Mark heard it over his police scanner, and then he confirmed it." Tessa tilted her head to the side. "What aren't you telling me?"

"And how exactly did Mark confirm it?" Oliver asked.

"Never mind that. Did you catch him or not?" Tessa dropped down into the chair in front of his desk.

"Yes, we caught him. He was on his way out of town, but we caught him before he could get too far. However, we're going to have to release him soon." Oliver sank down into his own chair and gestured for Cassie to sit in an empty one across from him.

"What?" Tessa settled her sharp gaze on him. "What do you mean you have to release him?"

"It's not up to me, Tessa. It's up to the law. You know that," Oliver grumbled.

"How about you just be straight with us and tell us what's going on?" Tessa leaned forward in her chair. "Every detail you can, please."

"He has an alibi, which means that we have nothing to hold him on." Oliver shrugged. "Trust me, I wanted this all to be over, but it turns out it's not."

"What about the bloody clothes that we found? You can't have an explanation for that. Are you having them tested for Richard's DNA?" Tessa's tone grew urgent. "You can't just let him walk out of here!"

"I had them tested, all right, and it's not blood. It's paint. Kirk explained that he's been doing a side job painting a house nearby," Oliver said.

"So, he's not the killer." Tessa nodded. "Here I thought this might be all wrapped up and done with, but I guess I was wrong."

"You had every reason to believe he might have been the murderer but the facts don't line up. There's just no proof. I'm not completely eliminating him as a suspect, but I do have to release him. I've got nothing to hold him on, and I'm pretty convinced he didn't do this." Oliver sat back in his chair. "Sorry to disappoint you."

"Wait. If he's not the murderer, then why did he run from us?" Cassie asked.

"Well, even if he's not the murderer, that doesn't mean he's not a criminal. I suspect he might still be the thief and the person who's been causing all the damage around town," Tessa said.

"I can see why you would suspect that, but unless you have proof or you want to tell me about Mark's source, there's nothing I can do about that until I get something more." Oliver clasped his hands together. "I'll be continuing an investigation into Kirk, that's for sure, but I still don't have any reason to hold him."

"And you're confident about his alibi?" Cassie asked. "Maybe he's paying someone to say he was with them."

"It's possible. The person he claimed to be with isn't exactly the most reliable, but I have Kirk's truck on a traffic camera near where he said he was. So, unless he could teleport or someone else was driving his truck, I think it's pretty solid." Oliver tapped his hand against the desk. "I know it's not what you want to hear, but it's all I have at the moment."

"It's a stretch, you're right, but it's possible someone else was driving his truck." Tessa pursed her lips as she considered it.

"I received confirmation Kirk was with someone nearby. Just not reliable confirmation due to the source's history and him being a family member."

Oliver glanced at the file on his desk. "I'm not dropping it entirely, but right now I'm more concerned with exactly who knew Richard was at that farm. There were no incoming or outgoing phone calls on his phone to indicate he had any communication with anyone the previous day after Simon had asked him to go out there. When I pressed Simon, he insisted he didn't tell anyone else. But someone had to know."

"Dean knew." Tessa crossed her arms. "But I'm willing to bet he's not the only one."

"Wait, what about the piece of material? Have you found out anything about that?" Cassie recalled the towel on the toolbox at Brent's farm.

"Not really. It's hard to pin down due to it being stomped on by Gerry. But the techs are still evaluating it. It's a small sample, not a lot to go on." Oliver met her eyes. "And it might be completely irrelevant to the murder."

"Any thoughts on what it might be?" Tessa asked.

"Could be torn from a towel, or a shirt, or something?" Oliver shrugged.

"And Candy's alibi?" Tessa asked.

"I contacted her, and she claims she wasn't anywhere near Little Leaf Creek at the time of the murder. But we can't verify it." Oliver had a sip of his coffee. "But really, the chances of her being in town and killing Richard on Simon's farm seems like a stretch. But I'm not ruling it out. There's still a lot to look into in all of this."

"All right, you keep working on it. Cassie and I have somewhere to be." Tessa led Cassie toward the door.

"Tessa." Oliver stood up behind his desk. "I know you won't leave this alone. If you come up with anything, let me know. I could really use all the information I can get. I'm hitting dead ends, and the whole town is outraged about the murder and the vandalism."

"Don't worry, Ollie." Tessa turned back to meet his eyes. "I've got your back every step of the way."

"Thanks." Oliver sank back down into his chair, then picked up the phone on his desk to make a call.

Cassie smiled to herself as she stepped out into the hall. Being able to witness a genuine moment between Tessa and Oliver gave her a window into what they both could be like when they managed to let their guard down. Cassie could tell that Oliver still looked at Tessa as a mentor. But things often got heated when he felt as if Tessa was stepping on his toes. It was a fine line for Tessa to navigate and she often overstepped.

"We don't have anywhere to be. What do you have in mind?" Cassie followed Tessa out of the police station to the jeep.

"I'm planning to get some answers." Tessa sat down in the driver's seat. She started the engine as Cassie slid into the passenger seat.

"From who?"

"Dean, the mechanic. I felt like he was hiding something. Whether he's the killer or not, I want to try to find out more from him."

CHAPTER 15

Tessa turned into the parking lot of the small auto shop. Despite the closed sign in the window, she noticed a car parked near the open garage doors.

"I think Dean might be here. Let's get to him before he notices we've arrived and gets prepared." Tessa parked and quickly stepped out of the jeep.

Cassie followed suit, though her panicked expression indicated she hadn't expected everything to be rushed.

Tessa hurried toward the open garage door. She'd just reached the door when she heard a loud voice she didn't recognize from around the corner of the building. "You did this! You need to tell them what you know before I get locked up for murder."

"Chill, relax. You said you had an alibi, so what's the big deal?" Dean replied at a quieter level.

Tessa put her finger to her lips, then gestured for Cassie to follow her to the corner of the building.

"So what? My alibi is Big Billy. He's not going to talk to the cops, and the cops wouldn't believe him even if he did. It's garbage, and you know it. Even if I had the best alibi in the world, those cops can still pin this on me if they want to. Look, I freaked out after I stole that horse trailer. I almost got caught. So, after that I refused to do some of the stuff the guy wanted me to. He was taking it too far, and he must have gotten someone else to do some of the things, but now I'm still in the middle of all this. You did this to me. Why did you get me mixed up in this?"

"Oh, don't act like you weren't begging me for something to keep you going. You're about to lose your place from not paying taxes if they don't condemn it first. You needed help. I tried to help. You can't blame me for this, Kirk." Dean's voice grew louder.

Cassie glanced at Tessa at the mention of Kirk's name.

"You're the one who told me where to go. You're the one who hooked me up with that crazy guy in the first place. It's your fault." Kirk barked his words.

"It's not! I told you a guy was looking for someone to do some dirty work, didn't I? I never told you it wouldn't be risky. Whatever you two put together from there is your business. I don't want to have anything to do with any of it." Dean lowered his voice slightly. "You didn't kill Richard, did you? I never pinned you as a murderer."

"No, I didn't kill him! You know I didn't. I'm not a killer. Maybe you did it. Maybe you wanted to get rid of your competition," Kirk snarled.

"I would never kill anyone," Dean hissed. "I'm not a criminal. Not like you."

A grumble of words too quiet to be understood increased the tension in the air.

"Best thing you can do is get out of town, Kirk. Get as far as you can. If you do that, you might be able to get out of this mess," Dean said.

"I wouldn't recommend that." Tessa stepped around the corner of the building.

"What are you doing here?" Kirk looked at Tessa, then Cassie as she stepped around the side of the building to join her. "Are you stalking me?"

"We're just here to find out the truth, Kirk." Tessa smiled. "We just overheard some pretty interesting confessions. Would you like to tell us more about this man you work for?"

"I'll tell you exactly what I want to say!" Kirk stalked toward Tessa.

Dean quickly flung his arm out between Kirk and Tessa to stop his approach and pointed toward the street. "Get out of here, Kirk! You're only making things worse for yourself!"

"No, Dean, you made things worse for me. You did it!" Kirk bolted around the side of the building.

"Thanks." Tessa eyed Dean as he looked back at her. "But I can handle myself."

"Sure you can. I don't know why you keep sticking your nose into things that have nothing to do with you." Dean looked past Tessa at Cassie. "Don't you ever think about the risk you're taking?"

"It's a risk we're choosing to take." Cassie crossed her arms. "Unlike all of the farmers around here who have been dealing with sabotage and theft. We know now that you have a lot to do with that. If it wasn't Kirk causing all the damage, who was it?"

"I have no idea." Dean groaned as he rubbed his hand along his shoulder. "I know better. I stay out of things."

"It sure seemed like Kirk thought you were in

the middle of it all." Tessa watched as Dean walked over to a tire, then stopped.

"Kirk is never going to do anything better with his life. He's always after that quick buck, but he can't hold down a job. So, if I hear about an opportunity, I might pass that information along. Nothing illegal about that," Dean said.

"Maybe not. But you didn't think it was wrong that whoever Kirk was working for was destroying people's lives?" Cassie raised her eyebrows.

"Listen, I didn't know anything about that. This guy came to me and offered me some work. I refused, but suggested someone who could do the job. That's all. It's just business." Dean reached down for the tire with his right hand, then cringed, and shied away from it, then he picked it up onto its side with his other hand and started rolling it along the ground.

"Did you hurt yourself?" Tessa followed him toward the garage door.

"About a year ago. Ever since I injured my rotator cuff, it's hard to do even the easiest task when it's aggravated. I was working on a car and I slipped and wrenched my arm pretty badly. I thought it was broken, but according to the doctor I just did a lot of damage. It slows me down, but I can still do just about everything I need to."

"I'm sorry that happened. It must have been very painful," Cassie said.

"Was, and still is. If I'm not careful, and I put too much pressure on it, it can leave my arm pretty much immobile for days. When I flung out my arm to stop Kirk from getting to you, the sudden movement sent the muscles into a fit. I try to use my left arm as much as I can but sometimes I forget." Dean sighed as he laid the tire down. "Look, I know you're both here because you think I'm holding something back from you. The truth is that yes I am. I'm not going to tell you who hired Kirk, and there's nothing you can do to change that. You're just wasting time none of us has. So, please, just leave me alone. I don't want to hear anything more about Richard, or the vandalism. I just want to work in peace. Is that too much to ask?"

"Don't you care that the person who killed Richard is taken off the street? What you know could help lead to the truth?" Tessa stepped closer to Dean.

"Look, it wasn't me. Just leave me out of this." Dean waved his hand through the air, then yelped at the sudden movement.

Cassie patted Tessa's shoulder. "This is pointless. He's not going to tell us anything else."

"Listen to your friend." Dean looked between the two of them. "You're getting yourselves into something you shouldn't. That's all I can tell you. I'm sure that Richard would have appreciated that warning."

CHAPTER 16

"Do you believe him?" Cassie glanced over at Tessa as she started the jeep.

"Kirk? Do you think he refused to do some of the things that were asked of him and someone else must have done them?"

"I think so. Why would he say he refused if he didn't? I doubt he has anything to prove to Dean." Tessa tapped her fingertips against the steering wheel. "I feel like we're spinning our wheels. We have a lot of information, but nothing to actually move forward with. We need something solid to start making this investigation make sense." She turned onto their street, Little Leaf Way, and rolled slowly onto her driveway. "We'd better hope Kirk is as innocent of the murder as he claims because I doubt he's going to stick around town now, and even with his admissions, there isn't enough for Ollie to act on."

"If only we could catch this person in the act, we'd have indisputable proof." Cassie stepped out of the jeep and spotted Sebastian on the front porch of their house.

"Cassie, you're exactly right." Tessa stepped out of the jeep on the other side and waved to Sebastian as he walked toward them. "That's exactly what we need to do. We need to set a trap."

"A trap?" Sebastian joined them in Tessa's driveway. He pulled Cassie into a warm hug. "What kind of trap are you planning to set?"

"A trap to catch whoever has been vandalizing the machinery." Cassie returned his hug. "We thought we'd caught the culprit, but it turns out he may not be responsible for all the damage." She explained the argument they'd overheard.

"So, you think there's someone else causing the destruction?" Sebastian looked between them. "And you want to lure them out?"

"Yes, or maybe catch Kirk in the act and get some evidence for Ollie. But I'm not sure how. We'd have to find a farmer willing to let us use their equipment and their farm. That's not going to be easy, considering this might somehow all be linked to a murder," Tessa said.

"What about your farm, Sebastian? Would you be willing to do that?" Cassie asked. "I'll understand if you're not."

"It's not that I'm not willing, but my farm wouldn't be the best property to use." Sebastian cleared his throat. "But Phil would more than likely let us use his. He's been hit before, so he wants this guy caught. I helped him out by repairing his old tractor, so he'd probably be happy to help us."

"If Phil would be willing, that would be great." Tessa began calling Mark. "I'll touch base with Mark about any legal issues involved, but we should get it set up as quickly as possible."

"Sebastian, why wouldn't your farm work?" Cassie watched as he began texting.

"What?" Sebastian looked up at her.

"You said your farm wouldn't work well for this. Why is that? You haven't been hit at all, have you?" Cassie asked.

"Because it's so close to town. It's almost surrounded by houses. It's not out of the way like most of the other farms. It's not an easy target." Sebastian glanced away. What was that? Deceit? She quickly brushed it off. She must be imagining it.

"That makes sense." Cassie peered at his phone as it buzzed with a text. "Is Phil up for it?"

"He agreed. We just need to let him know when." Sebastian looked up from his phone at them.

"I think we should try for it right around sunset. That's when most of the damage is being done. Too early for the equipment to be put away, and too late for anyone to be using it." Tessa checked her watch. "That gives us about an hour."

"An hour? That's not a lot of time. What did Mark say?" Cassie asked.

"He said if we can catch the culprit on camera causing damage or stealing the tractor, it will more than likely stand up in court. We just can't mention the other part of our plan." Tessa lowered her voice. "We're going to call our friend Dean, and we're going to get him to let whoever hired Kirk know that Phil just got a new tractor and he plans to test it out this afternoon. And then he and his family should be out for the rest of the evening. The person organizing all of this should be tempted into sending whoever the other culprit is to destroy it."

"That's a big assumption and Dean has to agree." Sebastian fired off another text. "But it's probably the best shot we have at making this happen."

"Exactly." Tessa hurried off toward the goats. "Hang on. I'm going to give some carrot pieces to the goats. And some treats to you, too, of course, Harry! We have these treats and we don't need them." She smiled and gave one to the collie mix who stood at the edge of the pen. "Mark said to make sure you know they're from him." Harry wagged his tail. For a moment, Tessa considered it might be from the mention of Mark's name. Then she pushed the thought aside as being ridiculous. He was just happy because she was giving him treats.

While Tessa tended to her pets, Sebastian pulled Cassie close again. "If you two are going to set a trap, I'd like to be there with you."

"We'll be fine."

"It's not just about that." Sebastian brushed her hair back from her eyes. "I want to be there with you. It's an important thing you're doing. Why can't we do it together? Besides, I think Phil will feel more secure if I'm also there. We've been friends for a long time."

"Sure, of course. Having you there would be great."

"Okay. I'll grab a couple of flashlights in case it gets dark while we're waiting." Sebastian went into the house.

"All right, I'm ready to go." Tessa returned to the driveway. "I want to get out there and make sure we can get a good hiding spot. I already spoke with Dean and he agreed to help us set the trap."

"He agreed, but that doesn't mean he'll do it. What if he tips the guy off? Dean's not a very reliable person."

"No, he's not. But he knows he has some skin on the line. He might not have directly ordered the damage to the property, but he helped facilitate the crimes, and whether or not he gets charged for that, I doubt he wants the police sniffing around him. I told him if he helps us with this, I'll forget everything I heard between him and Kirk and how he's connected to all of this." Tessa shrugged. "Of course, that doesn't mean the police won't fit the pieces together themselves, so he won't necessarily get off the hook. But that's not my problem."

"After seeing the amount of pain Dean was in today after just flinging his arm out in front of Kirk, I doubt he could kill Richard like that without having painful consequences. He wasn't in any visible pain the first time we spoke to him, so I don't think he hurt his arm killing Richard. But it's possible, I guess. I doubt he could have killed Richard that way with one hand. So, it seems less likely that Dean's the killer." Cassie glanced toward her house as Sebastian stepped outside. "Sebastian is going to come with us."

"You're right about Dean. And we might be able to pretty much eliminate Kirk as the killer because of his alibi, but he's obviously wrapped up in this somehow." Tessa nodded to Sebastian as they all climbed into the jeep. "Glad to have you along. You can hold the camera."

"Great." Sebastian grinned as he settled in the back seat. "Glad to help."

CHAPTER 17

After a short drive Tessa turned into Phil's driveway.

"He and his family aren't here, are they?" Tessa surveyed the visibly struggling farm.

"Just Phil. As soon as he heard what we wanted to do, he sent the rest off for the evening." Sebastian leaned forward as he looked over the farm. "Can't be too careful."

"Phil should have gone with them. We want the place to look empty like we said it would be." Tessa pulled her jeep around behind Phil's barn. "Wow, look at the state of this barn."

"I know, it needs a lot of work. Phil and I have been working on it piece by piece. It'll be sound soon enough. Trust me, Phil isn't going anywhere.

You can't ask a farmer to leave his farm vulnerable. Don't worry, he can help me hold the camera." Sebastian laughed.

"All right, but from here on in, you do what I say." Tessa stepped out of the jeep and closed the door. "No questions asked. This isn't a lark. This is a sting operation."

Sebastian hid his smile as he got out of the back seat and nodded. "Whatever you say."

"Cassie, help me find a good spot for us to set up." Tessa scanned the field. "I don't see any tractor out there."

"Phil keeps his tractor locked up in the barn now." Sebastian pointed at the barn. "I'm sure he's about to bring it out."

"Not a chance," Phil called out from the front of the barn. "I'll let you use my four-wheeler as bait, but not my new tractor."

"What?" Sebastian walked around the barn to meet him halfway. "You said you would help us out."

"I said I would help you out, but I'm not risking my tractor, Sebastian. You need him on tape stealing or destroying it, right? So, who's going to fix it after that?" Phil crossed his muscular arms. "You can't ask me to risk that."

"You know I would help you fix it," Sebastian said.

"I do. But what if he damages something on it that we can't repair easily." Phil unfolded his arms and settled them at his sides. "You're asking too much."

"All right, it's fine. We're wasting time arguing about it." Tessa walked between the two men toward the field. "Just get the ATV out there. If the vandal comes all this way, he's not going to leave without destroying something, whether it's new or old. And even if he just comes out here and doesn't do any damage, we'll at least find out who it is."

"All right, sure," Sebastian agreed.

"Cassie!" Tessa summoned her to the edge of the field.

Cassie took off at a run to catch up with Tessa.

Once they had their hiding spot set up, and the vehicle positioned correctly in the field, they all crouched down together behind a pile of broken fence posts.

"You're sure this is the best way to go about things?" Phil huddled down next to Tessa. "I find it hard to believe that he'll try to strike my farm with all of the investigating going on around town."

"If my suspicions are right, he'll take the chance.

It's the perfect opportunity. A new tractor, or so he thinks, and an empty farm." Tessa surveyed the surrounding farm. "But he certainly won't attempt anything if he knows we're here. Quiet everyone, and be still."

A few minutes later, Cassie covered a yawn and leaned against Sebastian's side.

"I'm going to walk the perimeter to see if there's any sign of someone approaching." Tessa kept her voice low as she spoke. "I know how to do that without being seen. You three stay put, and quiet." She nodded to them before crouching low and walking off.

Several minutes slid by.

Phil grunted as he shifted from his knees to a seated position. "How long are we going to wait?"

"Why don't you go on inside and rest a bit?" Cassie suggested. "They may not come at all, and as long as you don't turn any lights on and you're quiet, they won't know you're in there."

"Yes, I think I might do that. Okay, Sebastian?" Phil looked over at him.

"Sure. Just go fast so no one spots you." Sebastian tipped his head toward the house.

"Does he always do that?" Cassie peered up at Sebastian. "Ask you for permission?"

"What are you talking about? He just relies on me for good advice." Sebastian shrugged.

Cassie started to say something more but recalled Tessa's order to be quiet.

After a few more minutes, she began to worry about Tessa. "Don't you think Tessa should be back by now?"

"Shh. Someone's out there. I can see a flashlight moving. Be still. We don't want to spook them," Sebastian whispered.

As Cassie sat frozen beside Sebastian, she wondered if this had been a wise decision after all. The vandal could very well be the same man who killed Richard. What would he do if he found out they'd set a trap for him?

The flashlight beam swung closer to the four-wheeler.

"I have to stop him." Sebastian started to stand up.

"Don't." Cassie caught his arm and held it. "You can't stop him. We're recording, remember? We need him to take the bait, or we won't have anything to give to Ollie."

"Who's there?" the familiar voice hissed into the darkness. His flashlight swung wildly in their direction.

Cassie held her breath. Any chance he might overlook them vanished the moment he pointed the flashlight directly at them. The light blinded her for a moment, making her wonder if her first assessment of who he was, was correct. Of all the people she expected, he wasn't one.

"What are you doing out here?" Sebastian's voice took on an air of authority as he stood up.

"I could ask you the same." The man finally lowered his flashlight revealing his face to both of them.

"I asked you first, Brent." Sebastian took a small step forward and angled his shoulder in front of Cassie.

Brent the farmer. The one who had apparently been paying off the vandal not to target his farm.

"Cassie!" Tessa's voice carried from halfway across the field. "Are you two okay?"

"We're okay." Cassie hoped her response would prove to be correct. She looked over the man who stood in front of her for any sign of a weapon.

"What is this?" Brent started to take a step back. "Some kind of trap?"

"Yes, and you walked right into it." Sebastian nodded.

Tessa charged up from behind them. "Hands up, Brent. You're under arrest. This is a citizen's arrest."

"All right, all right, you caught me." Brent held up his hands as fear filled his eyes. Cassie knew that Tessa didn't have a weapon, but her tone was so authoritative that Brent must have thought she did, or he was so startled he just complied anyway. "Don't hurt me, Sebastian."

"Hurt you?" Sebastian frowned. "We're not going to hurt you. We're going to turn you in to the police for Richard's murder, the thefts, and the damage to property all around the area."

"Murder?" Brent gasped. "No. You can't do that. I didn't kill anyone."

"So, you and Richard didn't get into a disagreement when he found out you were behind the sabotage and theft?" Sebastian squinted at him. "Or was he paying you to do it and then he stopped, so you got furious and you killed him."

"I didn't kill anyone," Brent shouted.

"Settle down now." Phil's voice sounded from behind an overgrown bush just before he stepped out with a rifle pointed in Brent's direction.

"Phil!" Cassie gasped. "Put that gun away!"

"Drop it, Phil, now!" Tessa demanded.

"I'm not letting this guy get away, Tessa." Phil kept his gaze focused on the man.

Cassie could see the fury in Phil's eyes. Was he the person Sebastian was trying to protect? Could Sebastian's loyalties be misplaced? Could Phil have murdered Richard?"

"Phil, take it easy." Sebastian shifted his body in front of Brent to partially shield him from Phil's rifle. "Put the gun down."

CHAPTER 18

The tension in the air was thick between Sebastian and Phil.

"He's on my property. He's destroying my property. I have a right to defend it!" Phil lowered his rifle to avoid pointing it at Sebastian.

"What you have the right to do and what is going to happen here, are two different things. You know you can't hurt him, Phil. Put the gun down right now." Sebastian pointed to the ground in front of Phil.

Phil lowered the rifle a little more.

"Come on, Phil. You're better than this." Sebastian softened his tone.

Phil dropped the rifle to the ground. "Sorry, you're right, of course. I'm sorry."

Cassie watched the exchange with a rush of relief.

Tessa looked at Sebastian. "Don't let Brent get past. Show me what you recorded."

Sebastian gave Tessa his phone as he blocked Brent's path.

Cassie held her breath. She knew the recording wouldn't show much. Brent had spotted them before he had the chance to actually cause any destruction.

"Please, you have to believe me." Brent continued to hold up his hands. "I didn't kill Richard."

"But you did go around destroying and stealing property, didn't you?" Sebastian looked at him.

"But you don't strike me as doing dirty work unless you have to. You're the one who hired Kirk to cause problems, and when he refused to do any real damage, you took matters into your own hands?" Tessa squinted at him.

"I had to! I had no choice!" Brent's voice shook.

"You had choices." Phil growled his words. "You just made the wrong ones."

"Everyone around here thinks it's so easy to run a farm that's owned by a corporation, but the truth is they demand a lot, and if I don't show the returns they want, they'll come after me financially. And I could lose everything. I needed to make sure I had the profits to keep my head above water, and the only way I could do that was by sabotaging my competition. So, yes, I went around and did some damage to distract them. What else could I do? My crops aren't growing."

"You could have asked for some help from your neighbors. Instead of trying to cause them trouble," Sebastian said.

"Ollie's on his way." Tessa slipped her phone back into her pocket.

"Listen, please. You don't need to involve the cops. Okay?" Brent's voice faltered. "I didn't kill anyone. Yes, I stole a couple of things and caused some damage. I had no choice. My neighbors weren't exactly welcoming. I couldn't ask them for help. But that's not the point. The point is I didn't murder anyone. Please, if you don't turn me in to the police, I'll tell you exactly who told me how to do all this. I'll tell you who told me that Richard would be at Simon's farm that morning, and why they told me. I really need a chance to tell you my side of things. I promise, I didn't kill Richard. But I think I know who did."

"Why should we believe you after what you've done?" Phil asked. "You had plenty of other options, but you still put people at risk with your shady antics. There's no reason any of us should believe a word you say."

"Let him speak." Tessa folded her arms across her chest as she studied Brent. "He's new to town. We don't know much about him. Let's give him a chance to tell us exactly what he thinks happened to Richard."

"Thank you." Brent took another breath. "So, you see, this all started out pretty petty. I just wanted to cause a little chaos, make people more focused on keeping their farms safe than on having the best crop. I went to Dean and he hooked me up with Kirk. But things escalated pretty quickly because I just couldn't get the profits I needed. At one point I did ask Kirk to do more than I told him I would." He lowered his voice. "When he refused to do some of it, I told him I would do it myself."

"And?" Cassie shrugged. "That doesn't tell us anything about who the murderer is, unless it's you."

"Kirk told me how to disable the machinery. He explained that his deal with Dean was to destroy it to the point it would need lots of work, not be replaced. Dean wanted people to call him for repairs, not go buy new equipment. So, Kirk gave me a toolbox and instructions on what to do." Brent lifted his eyes from the ground to Cassie and then to Tessa. "The problem was a lot of people called Richard before they would call Dean. It made Dean really angry. When I heard Richard had been killed, Dean was the first person I thought of. He had to be the one who did it. His business was going under because of Richard. He wanted all of the repairs for himself, so he killed Richard. I knew Dean knew Richard would be out there that morning because Dean told me Richard would be. He said that Simon had called Richard out that morning to look at his tractor, and Simon was becoming very suspicious of Richard because his tractor kept breaking down. Dean didn't know I was the one doing some of the damage myself because Kirk refused to, and Dean told me I should make sure whoever was damaging the equipment would lay off Simon's equipment."

"That makes sense, I guess." Tessa looked over at Phil. "I think you'd better take that gun and go on back to the house. Ollie isn't going to want to see that."

"She's right." Sebastian nodded to Phil. "Go on, and make sure you stay inside until this is settled."

Cassie watched as Phil gave a slow nod, then he picked up his rifle, and strode off into his house.

"What's next, Tessa?" As Sebastian turned his

focus on Tessa, Brent spun around and ran toward the center of the field. "Brent!" Sebastian started after him.

"Let him go, Sebastian. I never called Ollie." Tessa watched as Brent sprinted across the field. Sebastian stopped chasing after him and turned to look at Tessa. "I had no reason to. We have no proof he was going to do any damage. I just told him I'd called, hoping he might tell us something more."

"But he didn't really. He pointed us toward Dean, but we already don't think Dean's a good suspect because of his arm, and we've pretty much eliminated Kirk as a suspect because he has an alibi. So, where does that leave us?" Cassie looked between them.

"Right back at the beginning. But we're getting closer." Tessa's voice was filled with confidence.

"I need to go speak to Phil. He's not going to be pleased that we let Brent go, and I don't want him getting hotheaded and doing something stupid." Sebastian gave Cassie a quick kiss. "I'll see you later."

CHAPTER 19

"Cassie, we should go." Tessa started toward the jeep. "We need to get to the bottom of this."

"Okay." Cassie followed after her and hopped in.

Tessa pointed at Cassie's purse. "Get your notebook out. Let's review things. I want to stop by the police station just to update Ollie. We might not have the proof, but we know Brent's the one who's been behind at least some of this, and he's not the murderer."

"Do we really know that?" Cassie flipped her notebook open. "Just because he said he didn't do it, doesn't make him innocent. He admitted he knew Richard was at Simon's that morning. Maybe he decided to kill him for Dean's sake or for another reason we don't even know about. Maybe Richard ripped Brent off and he wanted to get revenge?"

"It's possible." Tessa turned onto the main road. "But my instincts are telling me Brent didn't do this. He barely handled being caught and acted like a deer in headlights the moment we accused him of murder. I just don't know if he has it in him to be a murderer. But, of course, that's just my opinion and we need to focus on the facts, so keep him on the suspect list for now."

"Maybe we were too quick to eliminate Dean as a suspect? He could have been faking his injury just to throw us off." Cassie tapped her pen against her notebook. "We know Kirk has a pretty solid alibi, but it's not foolproof. But if one of them is the murderer, then why would they do it on Simon's farm? It would be foolish of them to do that. Unless they just lost it." She took a deep breath. "Or they killed him on Simon's farm, because they wanted to frame Simon for the murder."

"It would take someone cunning to do that." Tessa turned toward the police station.

Cassie's eyes skipped across Lewis' name on the suspect list. "Lewis is still a very good suspect. Sheila and Dean both pointed suspicion at him. He could have done this, he was furious with Richard. Maybe Lewis knew he would be a prime suspect, so he decided to frame someone for the murder."

"It's possible. But he doesn't come across as so calculated to me. I could imagine him losing it and killing Richard but not planning it all out. And especially not framing another farmer. Most stick together. But I've been wrong before. Let's pay Lewis a visit."

"Look at that!" Cassie sat forward as she pointed out the window. "A pink car. Clay mentioned a pink car cutting him off on Old Creek Road when he made the deliveries that morning."

"Oh, that's right. There aren't many of those around." Tessa pulled to the side of the road a few spaces in front of the car.

Cassie hopped out, walked toward it, and read the sign on the side. "Candy's Candles."

"Candy, as in Wyatt's friend who accused Richard of arson? That can't be a coincidence." Tessa approached the car as a woman stood over the open trunk. "Candy?"

"Yes." Candy turned toward them as her blonde hair shimmered in the streetlight that had just turned on.

Cassie guessed she was maybe sixty.

"I'm Tessa and this is Cassie." Tessa gestured from herself to Cassie.

"Nice to meet you. What can I do for you?" Candy sniffed a candle she held.

"We wanted to speak to you about Richard Lawson." Tessa watched her reaction.

"What about him?" Candy frowned. "He's dead."

"We understand you have some history with him." Tessa kept her voice even.

"You heard about that, did you?" Candy put the candle back in her trunk and turned to face them.

"What made you think he caused the fire?" Tessa asked.

"I don't just think he did it, he did do it, but it doesn't matter now, does it?" Candy shrugged. "When Wyatt passed away he left me his classic car that he'd restored. Richard was furious. I mean, what difference did it make to him? He got Wyatt's business, his house, everything. Richard didn't even care about the car. He just wanted to sell it. Then one morning I heard a loud bang. I came out of my house and the car was on fire." She clutched her hand to her chest. "And I saw a truck exactly like Richard's speeding away."

"What did the police say?" Tessa asked.

"They said it was an accident. Some sort of malfunction, but they would look into it." Candy nodded. "And then they got back to me and said that Richard had a solid alibi for the time of the explosion. I don't know how that's possible. He did it. He was there."

"Do you visit Little Leaf Creek often?" Tessa asked.

"I used to when Wyatt was alive but now only every few weeks. I deliver candles to the convenience store. The owner's an old friend. I'm usually here much earlier than this, though." Candy glanced at her watch.

"Were you in Little Leaf Creek on the morning of Richard's murder?" Tessa kept her tone casual.

"No. What is this? Like I told the police, I was home." Candy's voice wavered slightly.

"Someone said they saw a car like this out on Old Creek Road the morning of the murder." Tessa pointed at the pink car. "The farm where Richard was murdered is on that road. It's quite a unique car, wouldn't you agree?"

"It is, but there are others." Candy's eyes darted in all different directions as she rubbed her hands together.

"There are, but what are the chances? What

were you doing out there? The best thing to do is to tell the truth." Tessa softened her tone.

"What difference does it make? I didn't do anything to Richard. I wanted to speak to him because the police said he hadn't torched the car. I was following him, and when he stopped at the farm, I confronted him when he got out of his truck. I wanted him to tell me the truth. But he just denied everything." Candy sighed. "I was so upset, but I knew I wouldn't get anywhere with him. So, I drove away. Look, I never wanted Richard dead. I just wish he had let things be after Wyatt died."

"Did you see anyone out there?" Tessa asked.

"No. To be honest, I was so upset, I was in a bit of a daze." Candy took a deep breath.

"You should speak to the police. Tell them the truth that you were there," Tessa said.

"No way, I can't. I don't want to get caught up in all this. I had nothing to do with Richard's murder. I'm sorry that Wyatt's son died that way but these things happen, and at least Wyatt wasn't around to see it. Look, I need to drop these off." Candy grabbed a box out of her trunk, then closed it, and headed toward the shop.

"Well, that was very interesting." Cassie started toward the jeep.

"It was. She just happened to be near where Richard was killed, and she had a motive which she admits to. And she lied to the police about her whereabouts."

"But could she kill Richard that way? She's quite petite." Cassie climbed into the jeep.

"If someone is angry enough, it's possible. It can be amazing what people are capable of. She's certainly high on my suspect list. We need to look into her more." Tessa pulled onto the street as her phone beeped. "Can you check it for me, please?"

"Sure." Cassie picked up the phone and looked at the text. "Oh, wow."

"What?"

"It's from Mark. Apparently, Clay's late wife had an affair with Richard and she was on the way to meet Richard when she was killed."

"What?" Tessa gasped. "I had no idea."

"Mark said it was all kept hush-hush."

"There's our motive. Maybe Clay knew or suspected what had happened. We need to go speak to him."

"Wait, do you hear that?" Cassie tilted her head toward her partially opened window. "Is that shouting?"

"I think so." Tessa slowly began to roll through

the center of town. Her gaze turned in the direction of the loud voices across the street. "Is that Tom and Pearl?"

"It sure looks like them." Cassie opened the window more and watched as the verbal altercation continued. "It looks like Tom is doing most of the yelling."

"Maybe, but Pearl isn't backing down. Let's see if we can find out what they're saying." Tessa pulled into a parking spot along the sidewalk down from where Pearl and Tom stood. Not too close to draw their attention.

"What are they arguing about?" Cassie squinted in their direction.

"I can't hear. But whatever it is, it's getting more and more intense."

"It is. Maybe we can try to hear what they're saying if they don't notice us. But we don't want it to get too out of hand." Cassie gasped as she watched Tom take an intimidating step toward his wife. Despite being slightly shorter than her, his demeanor was very threatening.

"You're right." Tessa stepped out of the jeep and onto the sidewalk.

"How can you do this?" Pearl cried out. "He's

our son, Tom. He's our only child!" Her gaze traveled from Tessa to Cassie.

They'd been spotted. There was no chance of listening in to their conversation now.

"Is everything okay?" Tessa walked toward them.

"It's none of your business, Tessa," Tom retorted.

"Well, you're making a scene arguing in the middle of the street, so you made it our business," Tessa said.

"Stay out of this." Tom glared at Tessa and Cassie, then turned to his wife and raised his voice. "Look at the scene you've caused, Pearl."

"All right, all right, that's enough." Tessa stepped between Pearl and Tom. "Whatever you're arguing about, it has to end now. You can't go shouting at each other like that in the middle of town."

"Are you okay?" Cassie looked at Pearl.

"I'm fine." Pearl smiled a little too widely. "We just had a little disagreement. We didn't mean to cause a scene. We'll just be on our way."

"Pearl, why don't we go get a coffee?" Cassie reached for her hand. "A few minutes to cool off would be good."

"No, it's all right, really." Pearl wrapped her arm

through her husband's. "We'll be on our way. So sorry to have disturbed you."

Cassie watched as Pearl led Tom away toward a nearby parking lot.

"What do you make of what Pearl said, Cassie?" Tessa asked.

"About Tom being a good husband? About the argument being nothing?"

"No, not that. I meant what she said about Simon. She seemed pretty upset." Tessa looked across the street at the police station.

"She did." Cassie nodded.

"We should tell Ollie about the argument, and about Clay and Candy?" Tessa started toward the police station and led the way inside. "Mick, can you ask Oliver if he's free to speak to us, please?" She approached the officer behind the front desk.

"Sure." Mick spoke into the phone, then looked over at them as he hung up. "Go on back."

Tessa led the way down the hallway and opened the door to Oliver's office, but Cassie spoke up before she could. "You have to go out to Simon's farm and speak to Simon, Tom, and Pearl again!"

"Cassie!" Oliver walked over from the front of his desk and closed the door behind her, then turned around to face her. "I've already gotten reports about the argument. My officer overheard some of it, but he was in the middle of something and they'd left by the time he could go over to talk to them. There's no reason for me to speak to them again. It was just an argument."

CHAPTER 20

Tessa eased herself down into the chair and ran her hands along her hip as she released a soft groan. "Walking around that field was quite a workout."

"What field?" Oliver swung his gaze in her direction.

"Never mind. We have some interesting information." Tessa changed the subject and explained about Clay's motive and their conversation with Candy.

"Well, that is interesting. I'll speak to them again," Oliver said.

"And I really think you should speak to Pearl, Tom, and Simon again. I think there might be something there. Their argument was bad." Cassie winced. "It sounded like it was about Simon, but I'm not sure what about. We just heard snippets. Tom was very intimidating."

"Cassie's right. You must question them again." Tessa stood up from her chair.

"Are you telling me how to do my job?" Oliver snapped as he faced Tessa.

"No." Tessa tensed her jaw. "I'm just saying I think you should go talk to them. I think there might be more there."

"All right." Oliver's lips tightened as he eased back from her a step. "That's your opinion. But I'm the detective and it's my decision. So, leave me to do my job." He opened the door to his office and walked out.

"Ollie, wait!" Tessa followed after him. "I'm not trying to tell you what you should do."

Cassie hung back for a few minutes, as she didn't want to get in the middle. They had a complicated history, entangled with the grief of the loss of Oliver's mother and Tessa's best friend. It was clear to Cassie that although Oliver valued Tessa's opinion, at times he felt as if Tessa was stepping on his toes. She had a lot of experience and he would try and prove himself. Their relationship often became strained over the issue.

As Cassie stepped back out of the police station, she looked over at the corner where the argument between Tom and Pearl had unfolded minutes before. Was Oliver right? Was it irrelevant to the case?

Wondering what might happen next in their small town, Cassie sent a text to Tessa to let her know she'd be walking home. Sebastian had said he would be home for dinner, and some time with him would be good.

As Cassie walked toward her house, she felt a few locals look at her. They knew about the murder and probably about her being there when the body was discovered. And she imagined that many were worried about what might happen next. The sooner the murder was solved, the better.

Cassie reached her front porch and let herself inside. "Sebastian, I'm home." Her heart skipped a beat at the thought of seeing him as her thoughts were suddenly focused back on herself, her husband, and their marriage.

"In the kitchen!" Sebastian called out to her.

Cassie followed the sound of his voice accompanied by an appetizing aroma.

"Cassie, I was hoping you'd be home soon."

Sebastian turned away from the bubbling pot on the stove to greet her.

"It smells so good. Thank you so much for making dinner."

"You're welcome, but you don't have to thank me."

Cassie stepped up beside him to peek into the pot at the simmering vegetables and chicken. She was relieved to see it wasn't some sort of green concoction. "This looks amazing. You're such a good cook."

"Thanks. Healthy and delicious, I hope." Sebastian gently slipped his arm around her waist and waited for her to turn to look at him. "I can see something's on your mind. Did something happen?"

Cassie looked into his eyes. They were so welcoming. They always took her breath away.

"Quite a bit actually. I'm starving. Why don't we sit down to eat and I'll tell you all about it?" Cassie said.

"Great." Sebastian pulled her close and kissed her on the forehead. "I'll get us set up at the table. Why don't you go get comfortable? I know it's been a very long couple of days for you."

"And you?" Cassie paused in the doorway of the

kitchen and looked back at him. "With everything that happened at Phil's."

Sebastian put the ladle with a clatter onto the spoon rest as he twisted around to meet her eyes. "It wasn't the best experience. Phil can lose it sometimes. Hurry up. I want to have a nice warm meal."

"I'll be right back." Cassie freshened up and stepped back into the kitchen.

Sebastian had two bowls of soup, a plate of bread, and glasses of wine set up for them both, along with a tall candle lit in the center of the table. He caught sight of her as he set down the last spoon on a napkin and rushed to pull her chair out for her.

"Thank you." Cassie smiled as she sat down.

While they waited for the soup to cool slightly, Cassie told him about Candy, Clay, and the argument between Pearl and Tom.

"Oh, that's interesting. From what I've heard, Tom can be a bit of a hothead." Sebastian picked up his spoon.

"That I can believe." The first taste of the soup made Cassie even hungrier, and suddenly her thoughts were lost to raving about the soup and laughing with him about the bumps and hazards that occurred during the preparation.

By the time the dishes were washed, and Cassie had snuggled up in bed beside him, she was completely relaxed and was only focused on enjoying his company. She felt the safest she'd ever felt with his arm draped across her and the subtle heaviness of his breathing coaxing her toward sleep. However, as her mind began to relax, and her muscles unwound, she recalled the events of the last couple of days.

After seeing how angry Phil was, he was definitely on her suspect list. But she didn't want to push the point with Sebastian during dinner.

Clay had shot up on the suspect list now that they knew he had a possible motive. He had every reason to want Richard gone. If Richard had an affair with his wife and she'd died because of it, or at least if Clay believed she had, that was a big motive. With his build, he could have easily done the job. The more she thought about it, the more it added up.

"Shh, try to rest." Sebastian pulled her closer.

Cassie sighed as she reveled in his embrace. Moments later, she closed her eyes again, and this time she slept.

CHAPTER 21

When Cassie's eyes fluttered open the next morning, she looked over and found an empty bed. Sebastian was already up. This wasn't unusual. He woke up well before sunrise most mornings to tend to his farm. But he'd mentioned the previous evening he was going to sleep in, as he only had work to do on the farm later that morning, and the sun was still making its way into the sky. She sniffed the air for the coffee he would usually have ready for her, and detected no hint of it.

"Sebastian?" Cassie pushed the blanket back and climbed out of bed. After a quick inspection of the house, she realized he wasn't there. Maybe he'd decided to go for a jog or help out a friend, which he often did.

Cassie went through her morning routine and headed over to Tessa's house, knowing she would have coffee ready and would want to follow up on the investigation as soon as possible.

Cassie started to open the gate between their two houses when Harry barreled toward her with several loud barks.

"Shh, Harry! It's early!" Cassie gasped as she looked around at the sleepy neighborhood.

Harry barked again while Cassie fumbled in her purse for some treats for him. A moment later, as it dawned on her that he wasn't inside the house or the pen, she discovered the reason for his barks. The two goats, who she thought were still penned up raced straight for her and the treats in her hands.

"Easy, boys, easy!" Cassie gasped and managed to swing the gate closed to prevent them from escaping, but they ransacked her hands for every piece of carrot. "Nice to see you, too." She laughed. "I guess you were penned up a little too long."

Harry barked at them once and the goats bolted toward the backyard.

"You did try to warn me, Harry. Sorry I didn't listen." Cassie tossed him some dog treats, then hurried up onto Tessa's porch before the goats could attack her again.

After a quick knock, Tessa called out to her. "Come on in!"

Cassie walked into the house, and the aroma of fruit and sugar immediately hit her. Her stomach rumbled despite still being a little full from the meal she'd enjoyed with Sebastian the night before.

"It's time for waffles!" Tessa grinned as Cassie joined her in the kitchen. "I'm just starting on the batter and the waffle iron is warming up. I meant to have it ready when you arrived, but you got here a little earlier than I expected."

"I woke up early this morning. I'm happy to see the pets are running around free again." Cassie walked over to the sink and washed her hands.

"Yes, I didn't want them to have to wait any longer to get out of that pen. Sebastian fixed the fence last night. He must have done it before I came home." Tessa tossed some flour into the small bowl in front of her, then a generous helping of sugar. "Can you hand me that baking powder, please?" She pointed at it as she added a few dashes of salt.

"Sure." Cassie passed it to her, then leaned back against the counter. "How did your talk with Ollie go yesterday?"

"I managed to make him see, or at least I hope I managed to make him see, that when I give advice it's not because I don't think he's doing a good job." Tessa whisked the ingredients together. "It's that I'm used to mentoring him and I have years of experience." She grabbed another bowl, then cracked two eggs into it. "But I guess I should know by now that often it can come across as if I'm being critical of him." She splashed in some vanilla, then poured in buttermilk from her glass measuring cup. "I just worry about him sometimes. I always want to make sure he's okay."

"I think the feeling is mutual. Now that you're with Mark, he probably feels like he needs to protect you from being hurt." Cassie offered a small nod as she watched Tessa pour the melted butter from a saucepan into the bowl.

"I'm not 'with' Mark," Tessa snapped just before she began mixing the ingredients.

Cassie winced. "I meant, now that you're spending time with him."

"True." Tessa smiled and put the contents of the smaller bowl into the larger bowl and mixed them together. "Now that Oliver and Mirabel are practically raising a child together, I think a lot of the past of losing his mother so young is resurfacing for him. But to his credit he seems to be willing to work through it."

"Well, that's good. I think they make a lovely family." Cassie watched Tessa pour the batter into the waffle iron.

"So do I." Tessa smiled as the aroma of the waffles filled the air. "You know, hopefully Ollie learns from my mistakes. I was working so hard to be whatever he needed, but the truth was I couldn't be. Ollie had to figure out what he needed. It wasn't up to me. So, I wasted a lot of time and energy working hard to be what I thought he wanted instead of just being who I was and letting him decide what to take from that." She opened the waffle iron and popped the waffles onto a plate. "Get some berries. They're warm on the stove."

"Thanks." Cassie scooped some of the berries onto the waffle. "So, what you're saying is, maybe we try too hard to make things right and we should just let things work themselves out."

"Yes, sometimes." Tessa closed the waffle iron on the batter for more waffles. "Life isn't always as complicated as we make it."

"You're right. Often I think I should relax more about things." Cassie sat down with her plate.

"I wish I'd learned that earlier in life." Tessa

placed waffles onto her own plate. "So, where are we up to with finding Richard's murderer?"

"We were going to talk to Lewis again before we got distracted by seeing Candy's car. And I think we should definitely speak to Clay again."

"Clay just doesn't strike me as a killer. But I've been fooled more than once. I can definitely see Lewis killing Richard. Who else do we want to talk to?"

"Let's work out what we know and go from there." Cassie cut into one of her waffles.

"We don't have any phone record indicating Richard had called someone to meet with him. We originally decided that meant whoever killed him probably knew he would be there. That left us with Simon and Dean. Simon claims he didn't tell anyone else other than Dean. But we have pretty much eliminated Dean as a suspect due to his injury. Which leaves us with Simon. But he claims he was out in the field with his father. It's a bit like chasing our tails." Tessa had a sip of coffee. "We thought we had a good lead when we caught Brent at Phil's farm. I could be wrong but he also doesn't strike me as a murderer. And why would he kill Richard on Simon's farm? I think that might be a dead end."

"I think so, too. Though, it's still possible. We

pretty much ruled out Kirk because he has an alibi. Candy is still a suspect. She even admits she was there and that she spoke to him," Cassie said.

"Would she admit that if she was the murderer, though?"

"Maybe she felt like she had to tell us that because we found out she was in the area." Cassie shrugged.

"True. It looks like we can't really eliminate anyone, and we keep adding to the suspect pool. We should head out and see Lewis as soon as you finish your waffles and then take it from there."

"Most delicious breakfast I've ever eaten, you mean," Cassie mumbled around a big bite of her waffle. As she took her last bite, her cell phone began ringing. She glanced at the screen and saw it was Sebastian and answered it. "Hey, love, where were you this morning?"

"Are you with Tessa?" Sebastian's voice held a hint of urgency.

"Yes. What is it? Is everyone okay?" Cassie's heartbeat quickened, as she rarely heard any panic in his voice.

"No one's hurt, but there's been some vandalism at Phil's farm. Phil doesn't want me to call the police. I'm not sure what to do. I could really use

Tessa's opinion, and yours as well, of course, if you both want to come."

"Sure, we'll be right there." Cassie ended the call and looked over at Tessa. "Sebastian wants you over at Phil's farm. He said there's been some damage." She carried her plate toward the sink and picked up Tessa's along the way.

"To what?" Tessa grabbed her purse and the keys to the jeep.

"I'm not sure. He didn't say." Cassie followed her out of the house and hurried across the front lawn, through the gate, to the jeep.

"Phil was pretty angry yesterday." Tessa started the engine. "I can only imagine how angry he must be now if something was damaged."

"Sebastian said no one was hurt, which is good, but he sounded annoyed, to say the least."

"All right, let's get there fast." As soon as the jeep was out on the road, Tessa gunned the engine.

CHAPTER 22

Tessa drove quickly through town, then down the side roads that led out to Phil's farm.

"There's Sebastian's truck." Cassie pointed to the blue beat-up pickup truck parked beside the run-down barn. "I wonder if Phil lost his temper and went after Brent." She gasped at the thought.

"Sebastian said no one was hurt, though." Tessa pulled the jeep up beside Sebastian's truck. "Let's not guess at it. Let's find out."

Sebastian's head poked out from the barn doors. He began to approach the jeep with his hands shoved deep into his pockets.

"Sebastian, what's happened?" Cassie stepped out of the jeep.

"Come with me." Sebastian led them into the small, patched-together barn. "Phil called me first thing this morning. I wanted to first come have a look at it myself before I told you about it." He gestured to the new tractor that Phil had refused to use as bait.

Phil sat in the seat as the tractor rumbled.

"Someone did something to it!" Phil smacked the steering wheel, then turned off the ignition.

"It wouldn't start this morning, and I figured out the problem, but they've damaged the engine, and it's going to take a lot more work and new parts to get it fixed." Sebastian ran his hand back through his hair as he sighed.

"Well, calling the police to report it is the first thing we should do." Tessa pulled her phone out of her purse.

"No!" Phil shouted as he jumped down from the tractor. "Don't do that!"

Tessa stood her ground as Phil approached her.

"See, Sebastian? I told you not to call them. You told me not to do anything to stop the vandal. And now look what's happened." Phil waved his hand toward the tractor. "My tractor's destroyed, and I'm about to have the police at my door."

"Phil, relax." Sebastian stared straight into Phil's

eyes for a long moment, then looked at Tessa. "He's worried about involving Ollie. Not everything on the farm is up to code, and he's at risk of losing a lot if Ollie draws the wrong kind of attention toward him."

"Don't tell them that! She's a retired cop, and Ollie's practically her kid. Have you lost your mind?" Phil glowered at him.

"You can trust me, Phil, you know that, and you can trust them. I wouldn't have called them if you couldn't." Sebastian glanced over at Cassie and Tessa. "The lock on the barn was broken when Phil came out here this morning. So, someone got in and damaged the tractor. I know you're knee-deep looking into this, and I was hoping maybe you two could try to figure out who did it. If they're held accountable, maybe we can at least get the money from them for the replacement parts, so we can get it fixed as quickly as possible. Going through insurance could take ages."

"All right, then, we'll do just that. But before we start there, do we have any idea when the barn was broken into?" Tessa dropped her phone back into her purse.

"Yesterday, when we were out in the field. It's the only time I was away from the house. If I'd been nearby, I'm sure I would have heard someone breaking in," Phil grumbled. "I usually check on the barn before I go to bed each night, but I was so wound up last night, I didn't. I'm such an idiot." He groaned. "I sank so much money into this new tractor because the old one barely did the job and it's already broken down twice before. Now, what?"

"We're going to get it fixed." Sebastian clapped his hand down on Phil's shoulder. "We'll have it running in no time, and you're going to be fine."

"You keep saying that. You keep saying everything's going to be fine." Phil gazed at Sebastian. "But things keep getting worse."

"Just be patient." Sebastian patted his shoulder.

"I'm sick of being patient." Phil sighed.

"So, you mean to say that while we were waiting in the field for your four-wheeler to be damaged, someone was damaging your tractor in here?" Cassie asked.

"Yes, that's exactly what I'm telling you." Phil crossed his arms. "I never should have gotten involved. Didn't I tell you that, Sebastian?"

"You did." Sebastian rocked back on his heels as he looked the tractor over. "Maybe whoever did it knew we were out there setting a trap. It's possible it could have been Brent. Maybe he broke in while we were out in the field, but then why would he have come out there just to be caught by us?"

"Maybe he's just stupid." Tessa looked over the tractor. "But I doubt that. I think it's more likely that someone took advantage of our focus being elsewhere." She abruptly looked up at Phil. "We set the trap to catch Brent. The only other person who knew was Dean. Did you tell anyone else about the setup?"

"No one." Phil shook his head.

Sebastian kept his eyes on him and spoke in an even but forceful tone. "Phil, who else did you tell?"

"Look." Phil cleared his throat as he glanced up at Sebastian. "Some people have been wondering after what happened at Simon's farm, and all of the vandalism still going on, if maybe we needed to do something different. So, I might have mentioned something to Simon about your plan, just to keep him up to date on what was happening. But that's it. There's no harm in telling Simon, right?"

"Plenty of harm." Tessa frowned.

"Simon was the one who made the appointment with Richard. I suspect he told others about it. The same way he might have told others about our plan for a setup. Whoever he told is the key to what's happening. Maybe he told the wrong person," Cassie said.

"Now, I'm calling Ollie." Tessa pulled her phone out of her purse again. "Both the murder and this break-in have someone in common. Simon."

"Wait, I said no cops!" Phil raised his voice.

"Relax." Tessa met Phil's eyes. "No one's trying to get you into trouble here, Phil. We're all friends. Maybe you can help get to the bottom of all of this. You and Sebastian can even go over and talk to Simon. I mean, you're both friendly with him. Maybe you can see if you can find out more about his involvement. But just be cautious. Don't let on you think he might somehow be involved in all this. Cassie and I can see what we can find here. We'll look over the area and tractor for evidence."

"All right, that sounds like a good plan." Sebastian nodded. "Does that work for you, Phil?"

"I don't have much of a choice, do I?" Phil frowned. "What you say goes, Sebastian."

"You do have a choice." Sebastian's tone softened. "I'm just trying to look out for you. If you run off and do something crazy, I'm not going to be able to help you."

"All right." Phil's tone softened as well. "Let's go over there and see what Simon has to say."

CHAPTER 23

Tessa surveyed the interior of the barn, then glanced over at Cassie. "We need some certainty whether Simon was involved in all of this."

"Maybe Tom and Pearl can give an insight into that. But Tom doesn't strike me as someone who would give anything away, and after seeing the way they argued in town, I highly doubt that Pearl would talk. She's probably too scared to."

"I'm not so sure about that. Did you see the way she argued back? People argue. She was shouting right back at him." Tessa searched her memory. "They were fighting about Simon, right? Pearl asked Tom not to do something to him or something like that."

"Yes, it was definitely about Simon. What if Simon's the murderer and it was somehow related to that?"

"That's possible."

"Maybe having Dean out the day before and finding out it did look like Richard had been causing the issues with the tractor made him furious," Cassie suggested.

"That makes sense. Maybe it was a crime of passion, a momentary loss of sanity, perhaps triggered by his mother's harping about Richard taking advantage of his friendship with him. If Simon believed Richard was damaging his tractor on purpose, he would have been fuming and trying to get him to tell the truth. But if Richard was innocent, which we believe he was, he would have denied it and probably taken offence. Their dads go way back. Richard would have insisted he was honest. He'd been working on farm equipment and selling it for years around here with his father. He would have been livid that his and his father's reputations were being destroyed, and that people have been bad-mouthing him all over town, accusing him of sabotage and theft."

"The argument would have escalated, and yes, I

can definitely see Simon losing it and killing Richard," Cassie said.

"And that would explain why Tom and Pearl were arguing over Simon." Tessa snapped her fingers. "Maybe Tom wanted to turn Simon in, and Pearl wanted to protect her son at all costs."

"Oh, wow. I think you're right." Cassie nodded. "Maybe she would do anything to keep her son out of prison. What if Simon goes after Tom and maybe even Pearl to keep them quiet? They're in their seventies, or eighties, aren't they? How will they defend themselves?"

"We need to speak to Ollie and make sure they're protected. If he's a murderer, he deserves to go to jail."

"If who's a murderer?" A voice from the entrance of the barn drew both of their attention.

Tessa turned on her heel to find Pearl standing in the doorway.

"Pearl, what are you doing here?" Tessa met her eyes.

Pearl slid the doors shut behind her as she walked toward them. She rubbed her hands together as if to warm them as she looked them over.

"I could ask you the same, couldn't I? What are

you doing here? Who were you two just talking about?" Pearl offered them a warm smile as she spoke in a friendly tone. "I'm just curious."

"No one in particular." Cassie tried to keep her voice even. "Phil invited us."

"Oh?" Pearl nodded as her smile spread wider. "Yes, I imagine Phil would invite you here, considering he's friends with Sebastian."

"What are you doing here?" Tessa took a step closer to Pearl.

"Can't I just check on another farmer?" Pearl slipped her hands into the pockets of her jacket. "I heard someone damaged Phil's nearly new tractor. At least that's what he thinks. My guess is he bought a stolen one off Richard and now he's paying the price for it."

"Richard wasn't selling stolen farm equipment." Tessa shook her head.

"Sure he was. I saw him about a week ago, hanging out with that young fellow, Kirk. I just happen to know Kirk is connected with someone who deals in stolen things, including farm equipment. Kirk must have tipped Richard off to where he could buy some on the cheap." Pearl tapped her finger against the side of the tractor. "Everyone talks around me, thinking because I'm just a woman, and because of my age, I don't hear things. But I do."

"I think it's more likely that Richard was warning Kirk to stop stealing and causing damage to all the machinery around town." Tessa continued to watch her closely. "You see, someone hired Kirk to sabotage the equipment, and when he refused to do the worst damage, they started doing it themselves. Richard had nothing to do with it."

"So you say." Pearl glared at her. "But I don't believe it."

"It's the truth." Tessa slid her hand into her purse. She wanted to see if Pearl would let something slip about Simon's involvement. "Why don't you tell me exactly where you were when Richard was killed?"

"If you press a single button on that phone, your problems are going to multiply." Pearl grinned. "Just let this be a friendly conversation. We don't need anything to get out of hand."

"I think things are already out of hand." Cassie noticed the anger in Pearl's eyes. "Pearl, I know you want to protect your son. But this isn't the way to do it."

"Whatever he did, Pearl, you're going to have to let him face the consequences." Tessa kept her voice gentle. "I know that isn't easy. I know he's your whole world, and I'm sure that Tom wants to protect him, too. But what you're doing here is rash. You can't stop an investigation that's already reaching its end. Simon will be prosecuted for Richard's murder. Your best bet now is to find him the best lawyer you can and encourage him to cooperate as much as possible with the police."

"Oh, such great advice." Pearl smirked as she opened her jacket revealing a rifle hanging over her shoulder. "Now, both of you need to drop your phones on the ground and kick them over to me. One false move, and we won't have anything left to talk about."

CHAPTER 24

Cassie's heart skipped a beat. She felt her feet freeze to the ground. She never imagined that Pearl would be hiding a weapon or planning to threaten them.

"This isn't the way to go about things, Pearl." Tessa's voice sharpened. "You're digging yourself a hole here that you're never going to get out of."

"Am I? Don't underestimate me. I've practically run our farm for most of my life. I'm the glue that has kept my family together." Pearl pointed to the ground in front of her feet. "Phones on the floor, now. I can't have you calling anyone and interrupting my plans."

"What plans?" Cassie pulled her phone out of

her purse and put it on the floor. As she kicked it toward Pearl, she caught Tessa doing the same, out of the corner of her eye.

"When you're a woman, people think you're less capable. Especially among the farmers. Then you get to a certain age, and people begin to treat you even more differently, you know? They start to act as if you're a little stupid, or more than a little stupid." Pearl tapped the side of her head as she smiled. "But I haven't lost an ounce of this brain, and I know exactly what I'm doing."

"You're not going to get away with this." Tessa pursed her lips.

"Oh, really. Well, I think you've got that wrong." Pearl patted the rifle. "I'm going to get away with everything."

"It was you," Cassie whispered as she felt the warmth drain from her body. "You're not trying to protect your son. It was you who killed Richard."

"What's that, Cassie?" Pearl leaned a little closer. "Do you want to speak up a little? I'm a little hard of hearing, you know?"

"She's right," Tessa gasped. "It was you! You killed Richard! I thought you were trying to protect your son, but the reality is you've just ruined his life."

"He's the one who didn't get a proper mechanic to help him repair the tractor, isn't he? He kept going to Richard, no matter how many times I warned him. But that's beside the point. None of this is ever going to touch him. No one will ever suspect me of killing Richard. I mean, they would never guess that I could be angry enough to murder him or that I'm even capable of murder. But I was. I can do anything I set my mind to. And you two aren't going to tell anyone the truth, thanks to Phil and his faulty tractor." Pearl gave the side of the tractor a friendly pat.

"What are you talking about?" Tessa narrowed her eyes.

"They'll think you caught the vandal coming out here to cause more damage and he had to get rid of you two. So, when Phil's tractor brings the barn down, they'll blame the vandal. It will be a great tragedy that the two of you will die in the collapse, but none of this will ever come back on me or my son. It's not his barn. It's not his machinery. He's with Sebastian and Phil, so he's got an alibi. And you two won't be able to cause me any more trouble." Pearl kept her hands on the rifle. "I know it doesn't seem fair, and I really don't want to do it. I didn't want to kill Richard, either. But I will do absolutely anything to protect my family farm, our future, and my son. So, this is just what has to happen."

"You're not protecting your son." Tessa scoffed. "You're protecting your own hide, and you know it. You've never thought of Simon once in all of this. When the truth comes out, he's going to have to face the shame of having a murderer for a mother."

"Which is exactly why I can't let you go." Pearl looked from Tessa's rigid expression to Cassie's vacant stare. "Maybe it's selfish of me. Maybe I'm just trying to protect myself. But you two have left me with no choice. There were plenty of other people you could have blamed, or you could have let this all go. Instead, you dug, and you pushed, and you uncovered a terrible danger. You were going to make Simon go down for this. I could never let that happen."

"So, tell the truth." Tessa shrugged.

"The truth is I did what needed to be done." Pearl smirked as she stepped closer to Tessa. "You see, Tessa, you must have experienced everyone underestimating you all your life just because you're a woman. And it just gets worse and worse as you get older. You're not quite my age, yet, but you're close enough. I'm sure you already know what it's like to have people dismiss you or act as if you're incapable of something. Everyone assumes that I'm past my prime, that I can't be a threat." Her hands curled into fists so tight that the skin on her knuckles turned white. "But if someone takes a swing at me or my family, I'm going to swing right back."

"Except it wasn't Richard who took a swing at your family." Cassie couldn't raise her voice above a whisper, her eyes still glazed with shock. "He was trying to help by repairing the tractor. It wasn't him who was causing the damage. So, you took the life of an innocent man. You can't tell me you don't carry a heavy burden because of that."

"What burden I carry is my business," Pearl shot back. "Besides, how could I have known that Richard wasn't conning us? He sold Lewis back his own stolen trailer. I had every reason to believe he'd decided to steal from my son as well by giving him a stolen tractor and damaging and not repairing it properly."

"Every reason to believe it?" Tessa sighed. "And that was enough for you to kill him. You should have just gone to the police. They could have investigated the situation and found the truth. Then Richard would still be alive. Instead, you decided to take matters into your own hands?"

"Yes, I did. I confronted Richard." Pearl nodded.

"What happened?" Tessa asked.

"I went by the farm early that morning to drop Tom off before I went to the store. Tom had already left to join Simon in the other field, and I saw Richard by the tractor. So, I took the opportunity. I wanted Richard to admit what he'd done. So I took him some strawberries, so we could have a talk, and I could try to get the truth out of him." Pearl sighed. "But I didn't expect things to go the way they did. Wyatt and Tom had known each other for years. They'd been good friends. Richard had been friendly with Simon. I just wanted Richard to admit to the truth, so that I could prove to my son he was behind all of this. And I wanted Richard to make it right. Instead, Richard kept insisting he was innocent, that he had nothing to do with any of it. I just kept getting angrier and angrier." Her face grew redder with each word she spoke. "He couldn't even tell the truth and put things right."

"But he was telling the truth." Cassie's eyes

lowered at the same time her heart sank. All of the panic she'd been experiencing vanished under a strange acceptance of her fate.

"I didn't know!" Pearl shrieked. "I didn't know!" She cried out, then took a deep breath. "It doesn't matter now. What's done is done. Nothing can change it."

"Nothing can change that, but you still have a chance to change this. You still have the chance to make a better choice. You can let us go. You can change the terrible path you're traveling down. It won't end the way you think. This is your last chance to save yourself, to regain some of your reputation, and receive mercy from the courts because of your cooperation."

"No." Pearl spoke calmly. "The decision has been made. I hate to see the two of you wrapped up in this, but the time's come. There's no other choice." She reached into the deep front pocket of her coat.

As she did, Cassie noticed a missing patch from one corner of the pocket. Did her pocket get caught on a rough edge of the tractor when she killed Richard? It wouldn't have mattered if they'd been able to match the material. She could have torn it at any time. But now Cassie felt the puzzle piece slide into place. Panic built within Cassie as Pearl produced several thick lengths of rope.

"I'm going to make this fast, as I need to get out of here before anyone decides to come back. But keep in mind that if either of you tries anything sneaky, at least one of you is going to die right away. I doubt either of you is willing to risk that. I prefer the tractor does the dirty work but I'll shoot you if I have to." Pearl threw a length of rope to Cassie. "Tie Tessa up around the pole."

Cassie shuddered as Pearl pointed toward a support beam in the center of the barn, directly in front of the tractor. She could already see how Pearl's plan would work. The tractor would run into them, and the pole, the roof, and walls would collapse on top of them. Even if someone happened to rescue them, they wouldn't likely recover from their injuries.

"Make it tight." Pearl aimed the rifle at them as she watched Cassie wrap the ropes around Tessa's wrists and the pole.

"Now your turn." Pearl walked over to Cassie.

Cassie wondered if somehow she could tackle her.

"Don't get any ideas. I'll shoot you before you

can do anything to me. Well, actually, I'll shoot Tessa first." Pearl held the rifle under her arm as she wrapped the rope around Cassie's wrists and the pole, then tied Cassie and Tessa's arms together.

Hot tears filled Cassie's eyes as she felt the rope tighten around her wrists.

CHAPTER 25

"Pearl, don't do this." Tessa's tone softened. "There are lots of other options for you. Just let us help you figure this out."

"It's too late for that!" Pearl tightened the ropes one last time around both of their wrists, then she walked over to the tractor. "I know a thing or two about farm machinery. I've been working on our farm ever since I got married when I was only eighteen. I heard Sebastian explain the issue to Simon. It might be damaged but it will do the job." She climbed up and found the keys that Phil had left in the ignition. "It'll take a couple of minutes to start rolling on its own, which will give me time to get out of here. But don't worry, it won't be long after that.

Once it gets moving, nothing's going to stop it." She turned the key, released the handbrake, then jumped down and stepped away from the tractor.

"Don't do this!" Cassie shrieked as she pulled against the ropes. "Pearl, you made a mistake, you lost your temper, but this is premeditated murder."

"Only if I get caught." Pearl nodded to them both, then rushed back out through the barn doors. She glanced at them one last time as she slid the doors shut.

"We have to get out of these ropes." Tessa shifted her body as best she could and wriggled her wrists. "If we don't get out of them, we're not getting out of here."

"Maybe if we make enough noise we can get someone's attention nearby." Cassie stamped her feet against the ground. "Help! Help us! We're in here!"

"There's no one to hear us. We have to think of another way to get free. Once that tractor starts moving, it's going to pull that support beam down very easily, and then it's just a matter of seconds or minutes before the rest of the structure collapses. If we can get our hands free, at least we'll be able to shield our heads. Move with me, slide down low to the bottom of the pole."

"All right, I'm trying." Cassie eased her body down along the pole.

"I know the ropes are pulling on our wrists." Tessa grunted as she moved as well. "But we have to try. If we can get some slack in the rope, we should be able to untie it."

"It feels just as tight down here." Cassie sighed. "I don't feel any slack, do you?"

"No." Tessa gasped as the tractor moved forward in the direction of the pole. "Stay low, Cassie! It's going to collapse. Just do your best to dodge the debris!"

As the tractor rolled toward the pole, Tessa wound her fingers through the rope enough to reach Cassie's pinky finger. She grabbed on to it and held it. "We're going to get through this, Cassie. I know we are."

"I know we are, too, Tessa!"

"Brace yourself!" Tessa ducked her head as the tractor neared the center pole.

The barn doors burst open, and a figure in a hooded jacket ran forward. He jumped up into the tractor. The tractor ground to a stop right in front of Cassie's toes. She felt her entire body relax with relief. "Thank you! Thank you so much! You saved our lives!"

The figure jumped down from the tractor and looked over at them. The shadow from his hood disguised his features.

Tessa squinted to try to get a better look. "Please, can you untie us?"

He kept his distance as he looked them over, then shook his head.

"Please!" Cassie gulped out her words. "If the barn doesn't collapse, Pearl will come back for us. She might set it on fire. Or shoot us. You've helped us. I promise, we'll do everything we can to help you. Whatever you need."

"If I untie you, you have to promise to let me go." He took a step closer to them. "I don't want to have any cops after me, understand?"

Tessa peered closer at his face. Her heart skipped a beat. "Kirk? Is that you? I thought you were long gone."

"I was. But I need the money, and Brent wanted me to meet him here last night and show him how to damage a tractor like this. When he didn't turn up, I just got on with the job. I had no idea he was out in the field with you guys until he told me this morning. Then I realized that I lost my wrench when I was here. I think outside. I knew if the police found it they might find evidence on it, and I would be pinned for the crimes. I heard that Phil and Sebastian were at Simon's, so I thought no one would be here and I could try to find it. But when I got here, I heard you screaming for help." Kirk sighed as he looked away from them. "I almost left. I should have just left. But I'm not a murderer. I might have done a lot of harm to people around here, but I'm not a killer. I couldn't just let the two of you die."

"You did the right thing, Kirk." Tessa's voice held a faint ripple of fear. "Without you, we wouldn't still be here. I promise you, we'll make sure you're repaid for that. But first, you have to let us out of these ropes."

Sirens from beyond the barn sounded.

Kirk took a step toward the doors. "They'll come help you. It sounds like they're on the way here."

"But what if they don't get to us before Pearl does?" Tessa stared into his eyes. "You did the right thing. Now it's time to make the decision to keep doing that."

Kirk sighed as he pulled a knife from his pocket. He walked behind them and began cutting through the ropes.

By the time Cassie's hands broke free, she heard footsteps outside the barn.

Oliver ran in first with his weapon drawn. "Put your hands up! Drop the knife!"

"It's all right, Ollie." Tessa draped her arm around Kirk's shoulders. "He's the one who saved us. Put that gun away. You're not going to need it."

CHAPTER 26

By the time all the statements had been given, the adrenalin had worn off and Cassie was starting to relax.

"I just found out what happened from Ollie." Tessa walked over to her. "When Sebastian and Phil went over there to speak to Simon, Ollie was there, and when Phil admitted to the damage to his tractor, Ollie came over to have a look to see if he could find any evidence of who did it. He heard us pleading with Kirk to help us when he arrived."

"But he wouldn't have made it in time. That tractor was right on top of us, and they were still a few minutes away."

"I know." Tessa cringed. "I'm trying not to think about that. According to Ollie, the argument between Pearl and Tom was because Pearl was so angry at Tom because he believed that Simon had killed Richard and he was going to turn him in. He was going to turn in his son because he found blood smeared on the doorknob of the back door, but Pearl cleaned it off before the police arrived. Tom never suspected it could possibly be Pearl."

"What about Kirk?"

"What about him?" Tessa smiled. "As far as I'm concerned, he never said a word about being involved in any theft or vandalism, and he was the hero who rescued us. Isn't that what happened?"

"Absolutely, it is." Cassie nodded.

"The police can investigate, and if it leads them to Kirk, so be it. But I don't want any part of it."

"True. I doubt he's going to risk doing anything else illegal now."

"Here comes Sebastian. I'll let the two of you talk." Tessa walked away.

"Cassie!" Sebastian pulled her into his arms so swiftly that he lifted her up off the ground.

"All right, all right. Like I said earlier, I'm just fine." Cassie laughed as he set her back down.

"I'm so sorry I left you here. I shouldn't have done that." Sebastian's expression darkened as he looked down at the ground.

"You did the right thing. You had to keep Phil from doing something crazy." Cassie peered into his eyes as he looked up at her. "Was Phil who you were trying to protect?"

"Let's go sit." Sebastian steered her toward Phil's front porch. "Firstly, between you and me, I really was worried Phil was involved in Richard's murder. I know it sounds terrible, he's a good friend, but he was so angry with the vandalism and everything and he believed Richard was involved. But I couldn't tell you that and risk maybe Tessa, and then Ollie, finding out."

"You wanted to protect a friend. I get that, but what else is happening? Some of the farmers seem a bit scared of you." Cassie sat beside him on the porch swing.

"You noticed that." Sebastian glanced over at her. "It's nothing really. You see, when we came back from our honeymoon, and I found out about all of the vandalism and the thefts, the farmers in the area were understandably upset. They wanted to sit outside with their guns and look for the first chance to take down the vandal." He cringed. "I knew things could get out of hand fast, so I started making plans about how we would catch him in the act, stop him, and get evidence to take to the police without hurting him. Somehow that turned into me being in charge of something like a union of all the farmers. As soon as I agreed to it, people started spreading rumors about me, about how I'm so tough and they better be nervous of me."

"You would never hurt anyone," Cassie said.

"Exactly, but that didn't change the rumors." Sebastian wiped his hand across his face. "They got so out of hand, so fast."

"So, you're like the king of the farmers?" Cassie smiled.

"It's not funny." Sebastian laughed despite his words.

"I know you're the perfect man for the job." Cassie kissed his cheek.

"I'm not keeping it. Someone else can be in charge."

"Sebastian, look how much good you did. You kept everyone from hurting the vandal, and honestly, if someone had hurt Kirk, Tessa and I probably wouldn't have made it out of that barn alive."

"Don't say that." Sebastian flinched. "I don't want to even think about it."

"I'm sorry. But you do have a level head, and you're so smart. Maybe it wouldn't be such a bad idea to be someone who the other farmers around here can turn to for advice and direction." Cassie laughed as she poked him in the side. "You'll just have to prove to them that those wild rumors aren't true."

"It all seemed so stupid. I was going to tell you, but I was worried if Tessa found out what was planned, she might tell Ollie, and the police would try to stop us from trying to catch the criminal, and the farmers would be angry with me. They wouldn't trust me. Most are my friends."

"I understand. It's not a big deal." Cassie gave him a quick kiss.

"It's been such a whirlwind since we got back. I just want to relax and spend some time with you." Sebastian wrapped his hand around hers and squeezed it.

"Me, too." Cassie gazed into his eyes and smiled.

"Except I can't right now." Sebastian laughed as he released his grasp on her hand. "I have a job to do."

"A job? What job?"

"I'm going to go out to Kirk's place and help him with some plumbing issues he's having." Sebastian rubbed his hand along the back of his neck. "It's the least I can do, considering what he did for me."

"I'll go with you." Cassie stood up from the porch swing.

"Are you sure about that? He's not the easiest guy to be around."

"Then you can use me by your side." Cassie winked. "Besides, I know something I don't think you do."

"What's that?" Sebastian asked.

"We should bring treats for his dogs. When we were there last time Kirk drove off with them in his truck, but this time they'll probably be there. Mark said they were guard dogs, but they certainly didn't look like guard dogs to me. They looked like little fluffy things. But being prepared couldn't do any harm. And what dog doesn't like a treat." Cassie reached into her purse and produced a bag of treats. "I keep these for Harry."

"Good idea."

As they drove off in Sebastian's truck, Cassie watched the little town she loved so much pass by the window. There were all types of people in the area. Great ones, not so great ones, and even criminals who had yet to change their lives. She knew that there were many more secrets brewing below the surface and she was eager to help uncover them.

. . .

The End

❈ ❈ ❈

I hope you enjoyed reading *Broken in Little Leaf Creek*. Ready for more of Cassie and Tessa's sleuthing adventures? The next book in the series is *Skeletons in Little Leaf Creek*.

TESSA'S BUTTERMILK WAFFLES WITH BLUEBERRY SAUCE RECIPE

Ingredients:

Blueberry sauce

2 cups blueberries (or other berries if you prefer), fresh or frozen
1/2 cup granulated sugar
2 tablespoons lemon juice
1/2 cup water
2 tablespoons cornstarch mixed with 2 tablespoons cold water

Waffles

1 3/4 cups all-purpose flour

TESSA'S BUTTERMILK WAFFLES WITH BLUEBERRY SAUC...

1/4 cup granulated sugar

2 teaspoons baking powder

1 teaspoon baking soda

1/2 teaspoon salt

1 1/2 cups buttermilk

2 eggs

1 stick (1/2 cup) butter melted and cooled slightly

2 teaspoons vanilla extract

Mixed berries for topping

Preparation:

To make the blueberry sauce, put the blueberries, sugar, lemon juice, and water in a small saucepan. Heat on high and bring to the boil, stirring occasionally. Add the cornstarch and water mixture and bring to the boil again, then reduce the heat and continue stirring until the mixture thickens and it reaches your desired consistency. Serve warm or cold.

To make the waffles, whisk together the flour, sugar, baking powder, baking soda, and salt in a bowl.

In another bowl, whisk together the buttermilk, eggs, melted butter, and vanilla extract.

Add the dry ingredients to the wet ingredients and mix until combined.

Grease the waffle maker with cooking spray or butter.

Add the batter and cook according to the manufacturer's instructions.

Top with blueberry sauce and berries or your favorite toppings.

Enjoy!!

ABOUT THE AUTHOR

Cindy Bell is a USA Today and Wall Street Journal Bestselling Author. She is the author of over one hundred books in thirteen series. Her cozies are set in small towns, with lovable animals, quirky characters, delicious food and a touch of romance. She loves writing twisty cozy mysteries that keep readers guessing until the end.

When she is not reading or writing, she loves baking (and eating) sweet treats or walking along the beach with Rufus, her energetic Cocker Spaniel, thinking of the next adventure her characters can embark on.

If you'd like to receive an email when she has a new release, please join her cozy mystery newsletter at https://www.cindybellbooks.com.

LAKESIDE COTTAGE COZY MYSTERIES

A Murky Murder

DUNE HOUSE COZY MYSTERIES

[Dune House Cozy Mystery Series 10 Book Box Set (Books 1 - 10)](#)

[Dune House Cozy Mystery Series 10 Book Box Set 2 (Books 11 - 20)](#)

[Dune House Cozy Mystery Series Boxed Set 1 (Books 1 - 4)](#)

[Dune House Cozy Mystery Series Boxed Set 2 (Books 5 - 8)](#)

[Dune House Cozy Mystery Series Boxed Set 3 (Books 9 - 12)](#)

[Dune House Cozy Mystery Series Boxed Set 4 (Books 13 - 16)](#)

[Seaside Secrets](#)

[Boats and Bad Guys](#)

[Treasured History](#)

[Hidden Hideaways](#)

[Dodgy Dealings](#)

[Suspects and Surprises](#)

- [Ruffled Feathers](#)
- [A Fishy Discovery](#)
- [Danger in the Depths](#)
- [Celebrities and Chaos](#)
- [Pups, Pilots and Peril](#)
- [Tides, Trails and Trouble](#)
- [Racing and Robberies](#)
- [Athletes and Alibis](#)
- [Manuscripts and Deadly Motives](#)
- [Pelicans, Pier and Poison](#)
- [Sand, Sea and a Skeleton](#)
- [Pianos and Prison](#)
- [Relaxation, Reunions and Revenge](#)
- [A Tangled Murder](#)
- [Fame, Food and Murder](#)
- [Beaches and Betrayal](#)
- [Fatal Festivities](#)
- [Sunsets, Smoke and Suspicion](#)
- [Hobbies and Homicide](#)
- [Anchors and Abduction](#)
- [Friends, Family and Fugitives](#)
- [Palm Trees and Protests](#)

Road Trip, Risk and Revenge

CHOCOLATE CENTERED COZY MYSTERIES

Chocolate Centered Cozy Mystery 10 Book Box Set (Books 1 - 10)

Chocolate Centered Cozy Mystery Series Box Set (Books 1 - 4)

Chocolate Centered Cozy Mystery Series Box Set (Books 5 - 8)

Chocolate Centered Cozy Mystery Series Box Set (Books 9 - 12)

Chocolate Centered Cozy Mystery Series Box Set (Books 13 - 16)

The Sweet Smell of Murder

A Deadly Delicious Delivery

A Bitter Sweet Murder

A Treacherous Tasty Trail

Pastry and Peril

Trouble and Treats

Fudge Films and Felonies

Custom-Made Murder

Skydiving, Soufflés and Sabotage

Christmas Chocolates and Crimes

Hot Chocolate and Homicide

Chocolate Caramels and Conmen

Picnics, Pies and Lies

Devils Food Cake and Drama

Cinnamon and a Corpse

Cherries, Berries and a Body

Christmas Cookies and Criminals

Grapes, Ganache & Guilt

Yule Logs & Murder

Mocha, Marriage and Murder

Holiday Fudge and Homicide

Chocolate Mousse and Murder

SAGE GARDENS COZY MYSTERIES

Sage Gardens Cozy Mystery 10 Book Box Set (Books 1 - 10)

Sage Gardens Cozy Mystery Series Box Set Volume 1 (Books 1 - 4)

Sage Gardens Cozy Mystery Series Box Set Volume 2 (Books 5 - 8)

Birthdays Can Be Deadly

Money Can Be Deadly

Trust Can Be Deadly

Ties Can Be Deadly

Rocks Can Be Deadly

Jewelry Can Be Deadly

Numbers Can Be Deadly

Memories Can Be Deadly

Paintings Can Be Deadly

Snow Can Be Deadly

Tea Can Be Deadly

Greed Can Be Deadly

Clutter Can Be Deadly

Cruises Can Be Deadly

Puzzles Can Be Deadly

Concerts Can Be Deadly

MADDIE MILLS COZY MYSTERIES

Maddie Mills Cozy Mysteries Books 1 - 3

Slain at the Sea

Homicide at the Harbor

Corpse at the Christmas Cookie Exchange

Lifeless at the Lighthouse

Halloween at the Haunted House

DONUT TRUCK COZY MYSTERIES

Deadly Deals and Donuts

Fatal Festive Donuts

Bunny Donuts and a Body

Strawberry Donuts and Scandal

Frosted Donuts and Fatal Falls

Donut Holes and Homicide

WAGGING TAIL COZY MYSTERIES

Wagging Tail Cozy Mystery Box Set Volume 1 (Books 1 - 3)

Murder at Pawprint Creek (prequel)

Murder at Pooch Park

Murder at the Pet Boutique

A Merry Murder at St. Bernard Cabins

Murder at the Dog Training Academy

Murder at Corgi Country Club

A Merry Murder on Ruff Road

Murder at Poodle Place

Murder at Hound Hill

Murder at Rover Meadows

Murder at the Pet Expo

Murder on Woof Way

Murder at Beagle Bay

NUTS ABOUT NUTS COZY MYSTERIES

A Tough Case to Crack

A Seed of Doubt

Roasted Peanuts and Peril

Chestnuts, Camping and Culprits

BEKKI THE BEAUTICIAN COZY MYSTERIES

Hairspray and Homicide

A Dyed Blonde and a Dead Body

Mascara and Murder

Pageant and Poison

Conditioner and a Corpse

Mistletoe, Makeup and Murder

Hairpin, Hair Dryer and Homicide

Blush, a Bride and a Body

Shampoo and a Stiff

Cosmetics, a Cruise and a Killer

Lipstick, a Long Iron and Lifeless

Camping, Concealer and Criminals

Treated and Dyed

A Wrinkle-Free Murder

A MACARON PATISSERIE COZY MYSTERY

Sifting for Suspects

Recipes and Revenge

Mansions, Macarons and Murder

HEAVENLY HIGHLAND INN COZY MYSTERIES

Murdering the Roses

Dead in the Daisies

Killing the Carnations

Drowning the Daffodils

Suffocating the Sunflowers

Books, Bullets and Blooms

A Deadly Serious Gardening Contest

A Bridal Bouquet and a Body

Digging for Dirt

WENDY THE WEDDING PLANNER COZY MYSTERIES

Matrimony, Money and Murder

Chefs, Ceremonies and Crimes

Knives and Nuptials

Mice, Marriage and Murder

Made in United States
Troutdale, OR
06/26/2024